THE AMISH STRAWBERRY GIRL

AN AMISH ROMANCE

Naomi Troyer

Contents

Chapter 1
The Fall

"Couldn't you have waited for me?" Lavina Bowman cried out at the sight of 58-year-old Miriam Gerber climbing up the hayloft's ladder.

"Hush, I might be older than you, but I'm far from old. I can still climb a ladder," Miriam called back good-naturedly.

"I told you I'd get the seedlings down. The last thing we need is for you to break a hip, or worse – your neck!" Lavina was kind of kidding, but deep-down fear gripped her heart when Miriam's foot slipped on a rung.

"I won't break anything; now would you just stop nagging and kumm fetch them from me as I pass them down to you?" Miriam said as she reached the top.

Lavina sighed and did as she was told. If they had a greenhouse, they wouldn't need to keep the strawberry seedlings in the hayloft during the winter. But since they didn't, the hayloft was the only place they knew the seedlings wouldn't suffer frost. With the rising heat from the animals that lived below, it proved essential for them to over-winter the seedlings in the hayloft.

Ever since Lavina could remember, she and Miriam had planted strawberries as soon as the chill subsided each spring. Farming strawberries in summer and carrots in winter was their income and their livelihood. But with every passing year, Lavina couldn't help but become a little more concerned for the amount of physical work it required from Miriam.

"Here," Miriam said, handing down the first tray of seedlings.

Each tray contained twenty-four seedlings and there were almost a hundred trays in the hayloft. Lavina accepted the tray and waited for the next one. They wouldn't take them all down at once, they only brought down what they planned on planting each day.

She accepted the next tray and set it down on the floor when she heard Miriam gasp. Lavina turned to see the ladder wobble, but before she could reach forward and steady it for Miriam to find her balance and something to hang onto, Miriam fell through the air.

She landed on the barn floor with a dull thump, the sound not nearly as devastatingly loud as the fall could be to Miriam.

"Miriam!" Lavina rushed to her side and kneeled to search for injuries.

"I'm fine, I'm fine," Miriam argued as she tried to sit up, but she was in a lot of pain. Her face was pale, her eyes drawn, and a cold sweat beaded on her forehead.

"You're not fine. Where do you have pain?" Lavina asked as her eyes travelled over Miriam's body, searching for injuries.

"Everywhere," Miriam admitted with a sigh as she lay back down again. "Just give me a minute. My breath got knocked right out."

Lavina's heart was racing as concern made her own breath catch. Miriam might not be her mother by blood, but she had been Lavina's mother since she was six. Lavina could still remember the night her family's home had burned down.

She had woken up from the coughing, her lungs burning as the smoke created a haze in her room. Her father rushed in at that moment and scooped her into his arms. *The house is on fire Livy, we need to get out.*

Lavina remembered as her father rushed past the flames in the kitchen before depositing her on the lawn. He kissed her forehead and told her to run to the neighbors to call for help while he went back for her mother.

Lavina had barely made it past the barn before she heard the explosion. Later Lavina learned it was the propane fridge that had exploded from the heat. A lamp their cat knocked over started the fire.

Lavina had never seen her parents again, nor had she ever felt the need to own a cat again.

She had stood by the barn feeling lost and lonely while the bishop dealt with the firemen. Miriam had arrived to take her home for the night, but to this day Lavina had yet to leave. Miriam had become her rock, the voice of reason in her head. She had become the family Lavina no longer had.

The thought of losing her...

"Miriam, I think I need to call for an ambulance." Lavina couldn't stop the fear from seeping into her voice.

"Nee, nee. That isn't necessary. Just a few bumps and bruises is all," Miriam continued to argue, although Lavina could see that she was in a lot of pain.

Lavina reached out and laid a hand on Miriam's leg. Her heart stopped even as she went ice cold. Beneath her hand she could feel the protruding bone and the hot, wet sensation of blood. She glanced down and saw the barn floor stained with it. "Miriam, your leg?"

"I know. It took quite a knock," Miriam sighed, trying to catch her breath.

"Nee, it's broken!" Lavina rushed to her feet and went to fetch a coat she kept in the barn. She carefully wrapped it around Miriam's leg before she got back on her feet. "I'm going to go to the shanty and call for an ambulance. I'll be back before you know it."

"Broken, it can't be broken," Miriam argued weakly.

"Well, it is. I'll tell you not to move, but I have a feeling you won't be going anywhere." Lavina smiled weakly, trying to keep Miriam's spirits up.

"Jah, I think I'll just wait here." Miriam's face was growing even paler.

Lavina ran to the kitchen and grabbed a couple of quarters before she raced to the phone shanty. It was between them and the neighbor's house, almost 800 yards away. By the time she grabbed the receiver, she was breathless and her legs were wobbly from the exertion.

She dialed 911 and waited for the operator.

"911 What's your emergency?" a woman asked, sounding bored.

"It's Miriam. She fell from the hayloft and broke her leg. You need to send help now! She's bleeding!" Lavina rambled the words out.

"Okay, honey. Just slow down. We'll get help to Miriam as soon as possible, but first I need a little more information, like where do you live?" The woman no longer sounded bored, instead her tone was one of patience and kindness.

Lavina answered all the questions until finally she was told an ambulance was on its way. She ran back to the barn as fast as she could, but all she could think about was what if a broken leg was the least of Miriam's injuries?

Tears burned her eyes, knowing that she couldn't stand the thought of losing the woman that had become her surrogate mother.

When she arrived at Miriam's side, the older woman smiled weakly at her. "I've been lying here realizing you were right... perhaps I am too old to climb into the hayloft."

Lavina chuckled weakly. "Why don't I do the climbing from now on?"

"Sounds like a plan." Miriam shifted her shoulder and flinched with pain. "Ach nee, I landed on the seedlings."

Lavina couldn't help but laugh. Miriam lay weak and broken on the barn floor and all she could worry about was the seedlings. "I'm sure they'll survive. Perhaps the ambulance people can look at them as well."

Miriam reached for Lavina's hand and squeezed it tightly. "The only doctor they need is you. You have a way with seedlings Lavina, like I've never seen before. You'll nurse them back to health in no time."

"Just like the doctors will take care of you," Lavina promised when she heard the sirens approach.

When the first responders rushed into the barn, Lavina stood back and listened to the Englisch medical babble. She didn't understand a word of it, but she prayed that whatever diagnosis they were making wouldn't encumber Miriam more than the broken leg already would.

Chapter 2
A New Town

"Where are you?"

Aaron Richards tossed his bag down on the threadbare bed and smiled into the phone. "Zook's Corner."

"What? Where on earth is that?" his mother, Doctor Sally Richards, asked, confused.

"Amish Country Mom, Pennsylvania." Aaron said, kicking off his shoes.

"Are you on your way home?" she asked in her firm, doctor tone.

"Nope, not yet." He wriggled his toes and waited for his mother to begin her usual outrage at his life choices.

"Aaron, I honestly think you've played around enough. It's time to come home and go to college. You're twenty-three years old and all you have to show for the last four years is callouses and a vast knowledge of cheap motels and dirt. This is really becoming ridiculous. Your father and I didn't work this hard to see you throwing your life away." Before his mother could continue, his father was on the line.

As a lawyer, Angus Richards could play both the understanding parent and the firm disciplinarian. It was clear today it was going to be the latter. "What on earth are you doing in Zoo Town? Your mother is right, Aaron, this has gone on long enough. I'll buy you a bus ticket home so we can start discussing your plans."

Aaron felt the headache throb behind his eyes, like it always did when he spoke to his parents. Sometimes they would be in a hurry and just listen to his latest experiences as a farm worker, but other times, like tonight, when they had time on their hands they would judge and ridicule him for not wanting to become a lawyer or a doctor.

"Dad, I'm not coming home. Not yet. I just arrived here, and I wanted to explore this part of Pennsylvania a little before I come back to Boston." That had been Aaron's go-to answer for the last four years. Whenever his parents became agitated, he would ensure them that this was his last stop on the way home.

What they didn't know, is that Aaron didn't plan on returning to Boston any time soon. His parents had kept a secret from him his entire childhood and it was learning about that secret that had caused Aaron to get on the road.

It had shattered everything he believed about himself and about the life he wanted to live. Until he could find the answers he was looking for, he wouldn't return to Boston.

The only problem was his parents weren't aware that he'd learned of their secret. Aaron wasn't ready to shatter their worlds by telling them he'd discovered it by accident.

"I've heard that before and frankly, I'm tired of this. You're bouncing around like an immigrant, doing seasonal jobs on farms for minimum wage, if that. You're a Richards, Aaron. There are expectations that come with your name and your heritage. Your grandfather didn't become a supreme court judge to have his grandchildren waste away their lives. I'm cutting you off and that's final." If Aaron could see his father, he knew his father would be red in the face, his eyes wide with anger.

"Dad," Aaron said patiently. "You cut me off when I landed in Texas two years ago. I haven't touched my bank accounts ever since then."

Aaron wasn't sure if his father was angrier that he had issued an empty threat or that Aaron was paying his own way. "Don't you dare ridicule me; you're becoming a disgrace to this family. Your mother and I have used every excuse we can think of to explain your absence, but those are running out."

"Aaron, just tell us why you don't want to come home?" his mother all but pleaded on the other side of the line.

Aaron let out a heavy sigh, wishing he could answer her. Ever since he had set off on his cross-country journey, he had been asking himself just that. "We'll talk again soon, I promise. I love you both. Bye."

Aaron hung up and tossed the phone onto the mountain of flat pillows. Why was it that motels thought that six flat pillows would compensate for two good pillows? For a moment, he thought of his bedroom in the brownstone his parents owned.

Duck down duvet, mohair throws, and the best pillows you could imagine. An antique four poster bed set on a handwoven Turkish rug with lamps that cost more than a motel for a month to cast just the right amount of light at night.

Why did he prefer living in motels, barns, and farmhand bunkhouses more than his own home? Why did he choose to do physical labor for minimum wage instead of going to a reputable college to follow in his parents' footsteps?

Why did he still feel that hollowness in his chest that he had thought would dissipate after a year of travelling the country on his own?

Initially, he had thought that gaining experiences without his rich friends or overprotective parents would help him find himself. Having been raised in the wealthiest suburb of Boston and going to private schools since he could remember, Aaron still never felt like he belonged.

Once he had read on the internet about imposter syndrome, but he understood that wasn't what he had.

He didn't feel like an imposter in his own life, it just didn't feel like the life he wanted to live. It felt artificial, it felt materialistic and, more than anything, it felt shallow.

Was it wrong of Aaron to want his life to have a deeper meaning? Was it wrong of him not to care about his parents' money or his trust fund? He'd never discussed either with his parents or even his close friends, because he knew they would undoubtedly mock him. He could almost hear them if he closed his eyes. *You're set for life. Just go with flow and stop fighting it. You're on the highest wave there is, all you have to do is follow the instructions.*

But Aaron didn't want to follow the instructions. He didn't want to go with the flow and he didn't want to live off money that was more than he could need in a lifetime.

A life with meaning was what he wanted.

He just wasn't sure when or how he was going to find it.

Over the last four years, he had worked in eighteen different states. Finding seasonal work as a farmhand as he moved on. He never revealed his background or upbringing, otherwise he knew he wouldn't have been accepted by the men he worked with.

Most had no other option, others were illegal immigrants, and then there were those that simply lived for each season, never planning the next. Vagabonds or wanderers was how Aaron thought of them.

But he had yet to find a word to describe himself.

He wasn't a traveler, a seasonal worker, or a young man taking a 'year off.' He wasn't looking to do this for the rest of his life, and he wasn't looking for a better job.

No, when Aaron thought of himself, only one word came to mind.

A seeker.

Although Aaron was yet to learn what he was seeking. All he knew was that had he hadn't found it yet. Not even a sunset over the Napa Valley had filled that hollowness in his chest, or even a sunrise over an apple orchard in Maine.

One day, Aaron would find it, but until then, he would seek.

Chapter 3
The Dochder
She Never Had

"Eight weeks!" Miriam cried out exasperatedly. "That's preposterous!"

The Englisch doctor shrugged with an apologetic smile. "Miss Gerber, I don't have to tell you that breaking your leg is considered a minor injury after the fall you had at your age. It could've been much worse; it could've been a hip."

"A leg is bad enough. Surely, the eight weeks doesn't apply to everyone? Besides, isn't moving around good for the healing process?" Miriam all but begged, making Lavina smile.

They had spent the last five hours in the emergency care room to make sure that Miriam's injuries didn't extend beyond her fractured lower leg. After many scans and tests, Miriam had been fitted with a cast and was now being informed that for the next eight weeks she should rest as frequently as possible.

"It is," the doctor smiled indulgently. "But not when you're bound to climb into the hayloft the moment no one is looking. Am I right?" The doctor turned to Lavina.

Lavina couldn't help but laugh. "Exactly. Miriam, better safe than sorry. You heard what the doctor said. It's crucial that you focus on allowing this fracture to heal or it could bother you for the rest of your life."

"Pfft. Instead, I should spend the next eight weeks bothering myself. The strawberries! It's our busiest time of year. You'll never manage on your own!" Miriam cried out.

Lavina laid a supporting hand on her shoulder. "I'll manage. You've taken care of me my whole life. Now it's my turn."

"Well, if you don't have questions, I'll let the nurse call you a cab," the doctor said, handing Miriam her discharge papers. "We'll see you back here in eight weeks' time."

Miriam was about to argue, but kept quiet when Lavina shot her a firm look. "Denke doctor."

On the ride home, they lost Lavina in her own thoughts. Miriam sat fuming on the back seat, with her leg straight and her crutches beside her. Lavina was concerned about Miriam's recovery, but she was more concerned with about what Miriam's injury would mean for their harvest.

Strawberry harvests during the summer were their primary source of income. Although they didn't do too bad over winter with the carrots, it was the strawberries that afforded them a comfortable life. Many folks in the community were often shocked to learn that Lavina and Miriam managed the entire strawberry operation alone.

They worked hard, but neither woman minded. They enjoyed what they did and, they enjoyed doing it together.

Although Lavina had reached the age where she should start courting and finding a man to spend the rest of her life with, Lavina couldn't imagine leaving Miriam and the farm that had become her home.

Now she could imagine it even less. Miriam was growing older and if today's accident had taught her anything, it was that Miriam couldn't farm forever. Eventually her body wouldn't be able to cope with the physical work and long hours in the sun and when that happened, Lavina would need to be there to help.

She already couldn't see how she was going to manage the next eight weeks on her own. Between getting the seedlings down from the hayloft, the daily watering that took place during the first two weeks and then monitoring the growth and checking frequently for pests…

A sigh escaped her as the Englisch driver pulled up next to the barn.

"Let the driver help you get down the other seedlings," Miriam said, as if reading Lavina's mind.

"I will do no such thing. The only thing I'm going to do is to get you inside and settled in the living room. The farm can wait for a day," Lavina said firmly before she smiled at the driver and paid him.

Lavina kept one hand around Miriam's waist as she hobbled across the yard with her crutches. Lavina could see the exertion was making Miriam tired, so she stopped every few steps and gave her a chance to catch her breath.

By the time Miriam was in the living room with a footrest to keep her leg elevated, Lavina was a little exhausted herself.

"How about something to eat, then you can take your pain medication?" Lavina asked, noticing the drawn look in Miriam's gaze.

"I don't want to be a nuisance, but that would be gut. This leg is pounding from hopping about. I'm not a rabbit, I shouldn't be hopping," Miriam complained again.

"Then you shouldn't have climbed into the hayloft," Lavina said, tired of arguing and listening to Miriam's complaining. As soon as the words escaped her, she sighed with apology. "I'm sorry, it's just been a long day, and I was terrified when I saw you land on the floor."

Miriam smiled patiently and reached for Lavina's hand. "I'm not going anywhere; you can stop fussing."

"Just promise that was the last time you try climbing into the hayloft?" Lavina all but pleaded.

"I will, but then you have to promise me something as well?" Miriam asked with a hopeful smile.

"Anything," Lavina agreed immediately.

"Gut. Then you'll go into town and put up a sign that we need a seasonal worker to help you for the next eight weeks." Miriam lifted her finger when Lavina opened her mouth to argue. "You already agreed to anything. You can't possibly manage strawberries all on your own and even if you could, when do you suppose you'll rest?"

"But we can't afford a seasonal worker," Lavina argued.

"Jah, we can. Go to the sideboard and open the top right drawer. In the back there is a tin. Bring it over," Miriam ordered.

Lavina did as she was told and returned with the tin. Miriam opened it and revealed a few bundled notes inside.

"This is our rainy-day fund. We've never used it before, but right now, it's pouring."

"But… how?" Lavina asked shaking her head with confusion. She had never seen the tin before and couldn't imagine how Lavina had managed to save so much money.

"Every harvest, I took a tenth of every sale and put it away. We have enough for a seasonal worker for a year or more in this tin. So don't argue with me Lavina, just go and put up some signs tomorrow." Miriam said closing the tin again.

Lavina wasn't sure if she was in shock or if she just didn't feel like arguing anymore, so she nodded. "I'll put up the signs in the morning. What would you like to eat?"

"Eggs and toast? I'm not really that hungry." Miriam yawned.

Lavina smiled knowing that the day was finally getting to her. "Eggs and toast it will be. With some tea and an extra spoon of sugar."

Miriam smiled gratefully. "You're the dochder I never had."

Miriam had repeated that phrase to Lavina over and over since she had spent that first night in Miriam's home. She had later learned that Miriam couldn't bear children, and that was why she chose never to marry.

As always, she returned the phrase with one of her own. "And you're the familye Gott blessed me with when he called mine home."

Lavina made her way to the kitchen, but took a moment to wipe the dampness from her eyes. Today had been the first time she had realized that Miriam wouldn't always be there. Just the thought of losing her made Lavina's throat close with fear.

She glanced up at the ceiling and sighed. *"Gott, please let her heal. Please keep her healthy and safe and please... let us find the right seasonal worker to help me. I can't let Miriam down... Amen."*

Chapter 4
The Right Thing to Do

When Aaron had seen the job posting at an Amish farm, he'd kept it in the back of his mind, hoping to find something else instead.

But after a week of living in a motel and trying to find work as a seasonal farm hand, his options were becoming slim. It was the first time since Texas that he considered using his bank card. But he refused to give his father that satisfaction.

The moment he made a withdrawal, his father would know and be on his case about coming back home. Not that Aaron wanted to prove he could be independent, but not having to listen to his father's opinions about his life choices because he wasn't paying for them.

Instead, he finally gave in and phoned the number on the job poster. He'd been told to hang on three times before he eventually spoke to a woman named Lavina. Aaron wasn't sure what the circumstances were or why an Amish woman was handling the interviews instead of her husband. He just knew he needed a job or he needed to move on.

The option to do the latter had come to him a few times over the last few days, but he'd decided against it. Something about Lancaster County and the rolling hills made him want to stay a little longer. He wasn't sure if it was the peaceful town, the friendly residents, or the appearance of a buggy now and then, but he wasn't ready to leave just yet.

So instead he was making his way towards the Amish community on the far side of town. According to Lavina's instructions, he should walk past the large oak tree with a broken limb, then turn at the crossing with the red barn. After that, he should walk for about five minutes until he saw a row of pine trees where he had to turn left, then the Gerber Farm would be another six hundred yards up the road.

It was the first time in his life he was following directions of that description instead of punching in the address on his GPS. But the GPS didn't recognize the phrase Gerber Farm or big oak tree.

Spring was slowly giving way to the heat of summer. Sweat beaded on his forehead, even as it trickled down his back. Suddenly, he appreciated the appearance of buggies more than he had before. He couldn't imagine walking all this way every day from the motel. Perhaps they would lend him a buggy, he hoped as he finally turned at the row of pine trees.

For a moment, he stopped and couldn't help but appreciate the surrounding landscape. There wasn't a skyscraper in sight, or even a car. Instead, it was as if he had just walked into the previous century. Horses pulled plows while men with wide-brim hats held the reins. Children played in the distance with skipping ropes and what looked to be wooden trains.

A woman hung laundry out to dry, a strange white hat on her head, like he'd seen the other Amish woman in town wear. It was a different world altogether.

For a moment, his fear of the unknown tempted him to turn back and return to the twenty-second century. Instead, something in his heart made him continue towards the Gerber farm. If he was looking for life experiences, he couldn't imagine a better one to add to his collection that working on an Amish farm.

He stopped at the wooden sign that had the word 'Gerber' carved into it and glanced at the beautiful old barn. Although it was probably twice his age or more, it gleamed red from the oil that they had nurtured it with over the years.

A small simple house stood on the other side of the yard; a large wide porch looked welcoming from the afternoon heat. Aaron adjusted his ball cap and checked his phone, only to find he had no signal. He'd worked on farms without signal before, but somehow this time felt different.

As he approached the porch, the front door opened and a woman hopped out on crutches. Her one leg was in a cast and although she was injured, she wore the same plain dress and white hat as the other women he'd seen along the way.

"Are you Aaron?" she called out, leaning on one crutch as she shielded her eyes from the sun.

"Yes ma'am," Aaron called back.

"Kumm, you can wait on the porch while I call Lavina," she called back. If Aaron had expected her to call someone inside the house, he had been wrong. Instead, she turned her head towards the fields and cried out in a loud voice. "Laaaaaviiiiiinaaaa!"

Aaron wondered why she didn't just call her on a phone, but then quickly remembered after his brief research of the night before that the Amish didn't have phones, or electricity for that matter.

"I'm Miriam Gerber," the woman smiled warmly when he'd reached the porch. "You do not know how relieved I am that you've come."

Before Aaron could say something, he heard the same voice he'd spoken on the phone with.

"What is it? The way you're calling me, I thought you broke your head this time." Although the voice was teasing, Aaron could hear the affection.

"Aaron is here," Miriam explained simply. "Aaron, this is Lavina Bowman. Lavina, why don't you fetch some sun tea?"

Aaron couldn't help but appreciate how beautiful Lavina was. She didn't have a touch of makeup on and yet her lips were a dusky pink, her cheeks just the right shade of blush and her eyes the most beautiful shade of hazel he'd ever encountered. They weren't brown, nor were they green. Instead, it was as if an olive-green circle guarded the gold around her pupil.

"I'll be right back," Lavina agreed before she headed inside.

"Sit, please," Miriam insisted.

Once everyone had a glass of tea, Miriam turned to Aaron with a hopeful smile. "The thing is Aaron, we need help and we need it urgently. Usually Lavina and I have no trouble with the strawberry season on our own, but I can't help for the next eight weeks. Lavina knows every part of the farm and exactly how to grow the most delicious strawberries you've ever tasted, but she can't do it alone."

"Strawberries?" Aaron asked with a curious smile. "I've never worked on a strawberry farm before."

"See, Miriam. I told you I'd be better off managing on my own," Lavina quickly intervened, glancing at Aaron with speculation in her eyes.

Miriam cast her a narrowed look. "Eight weeks remember, you promised."

Aaron wasn't sure what the promise was about, but he could see Lavina sigh with acceptance. She turned to Aaron with a look that made it clear he wouldn't be accepting their terms before she stated them. "Room and board will be included. There is a room in the barn that you can use, and we'll provide three meals a day. It's minimum wage and although some days we work from dawn till dusk, we don't work on Saturdays or Sundays. We don't have transport, except for the buggy. We don't have electricity, cellphone service, or television, and as for your ablutions, there is an outhouse behind the barn."

Aaron was about to laugh when he realized she was being perfectly serious. Any other time in any other state he would have walked out before even considering accepting the job, but Miriam's desperate look clashing with Lavina's look of triumph made him smile. "Great, I can start in the morning."

Miriam laughed and smiled with relief, but Lavina frowned and sighed with trepidation. "You're taking the position?"

"Yup. Can't see why not? I've heard Amish cooking is the best and I am quite fond of strawberries."

Later, on the long walk back to town, Aaron would wonder why he had accepted the position so readily. He couldn't answer himself. The only explanation he had was that it felt like the right thing to do.

Chapter 5
A Doubtful Tour

"He's here!" Miriam called out excitedly from her position in the living room.

Lavina glanced at the clock on the wall and didn't want to be impressed that it was only seven o'clock in the morning.

After meeting Aaron the day before and having Miriam hire him right on the spot, she couldn't help but feel a little cautious. It was one thing to hire a farmhand, another entirely to hire an Englischer. She knew that the bishop and no one else would have any quarrel about it, given most of them hired seasonal hands as well, but Lavina didn't like the way he smiled at her.

Never had her tummy flipped upside down at the sight of a man's smile. Her heart also hadn't galloped into a racing beat at the thought of seeing him again.

She glanced through the kitchen window as he climbed out of the cab and felt her heart do just that again. The feeling was as foreign to Lavina as the thought of hiring an Englischer to help her with the strawberries.

From her vantage point, she noticed how handsome he was. The day before, she had been so fixated on convincing her aunt that they shouldn't hire him, that now that she had a chance, she took her time to look him over.

His hair, that had been hidden beneath a ball cap the day before, was trimmed short. Even from across the yard, she could see his green eyes. They were bright and friendly and made her want to take a closer inspection to pin down the shade. Aaron's shoulders were broad, like most of the men in her community; it spoke of hard work, and she had to respect that.

He hoisted the large duffel bag onto his shoulder and approached the house.

For a moment, their gazes met through the window.

Lavina felt a rush of heat race into her cheeks before she glanced away. A few moments later, she heard his footsteps on the porch.

After thirty minutes of Miriam discussing what they needed from Aaron, Lavina showed him to the room in the barn. As she turned to give him a moment to settle in, she smelled his cologne. It was fresh and clean, not overly heady, like some of the Englischers she had met in town.

"I'll… I'll wait for you on the porch, then we can start," Lavina said quickly before she made her way out of the barn.

She took a seat on the porch and wondered why she was acting so strangely around him. For the first time, she wished she had a sister whom she could ask. But deep down Lavina knew what the answer would be. She was attracted to him.

It made little sense. He was a seasonal farmhand, nothing more.

And an Englischer!

"Right, teach me about strawberries," Aaron said, coming around the porch.

Lavina stood up and summoned a smile. "Let's go."

"I like your accent," Aaron commented as he followed her back to the barn.

"It's Dutch. Pennsylvania Dutch," Lavina explained.

"It's nice," Aaron repeated. "Do you speak Dutch?"

"Most of the time I don't, but I can. My parents taught me when I was young," Lavina explained as she stopped inside the barn.

"Your mother seems really nice."

The stab was unexpected and sharp. "Miriam… Miriam isn't my mamm. Not my real mamm, anyway. She took me in when I was six. I don't have any other familye except for her."

Aaron's brow furrowed with sympathy. "I'm so sorry, I just thought… my mistake. Just like I mistook you for posting the ad on your husband's behalf."

"Husband?" Lavina asked, confused.

"Yeah, I thought you had a husband." Aaron chuckled. "My mistake."

Lavina wasn't sure if it was relief or curiosity in his gaze. There were so many unanswered questions in her mind about him, perhaps in time she would be answer at least a few of them.

She drew in a deep breath and began the spiel she had prepared the night before. "Right, we keep the seedlings in the hayloft. This time of year, they're ready to be planted. We've fallen behind with planting, so the sooner we get the seedlings in the ground, the better."

"Need me to bring them down?" Aaron asked, already aiming for the ladder.

"Nee!" Lavina quickly stopped him. "I mean, not now. Let me show you the fields first."

After showing him the fields and the different stages of plants they had, Lavina led him back to the barn. "Now I think I told you everything I should, but if you have a question, just ask."

"Is caring for the barn animals part of my job?" Aaron asked. He leaned into the stable and scratched the horse's head. Usually that mare didn't much like strangers, but she leaned into Aaron's hand is if it were her lifeline.

"Nee, it's all right. I manage," Lavina answered his question.

Aaron retrieved his hand and searched her gaze. "Lavina, I'm not here to make sure you manage. I'm here to help. I know how much work mucking out a stall can be. How about I muck out the stalls and you feed and water the horses?"

"Are you sure? I... I can't pay you extra..." Lavina said under her breath.

"You don't have to. Since we're going to be roommates, I'd like them to be clean," Aaron chuckled. "I meant the horses."

Lavina smiled. "Denke, I'd appreciate that." She glanced at the clock on the wall and let out a sigh. "It's time for Miriam's medicine. Do you want to come up to the house for a snack while I give it to her?"

"No," Aaron shook his head. "I think I'll get started."

Lavina wasn't about to disagree. When she returned to the barn almost an hour later, it surprised her to see how many seed trays he'd brought down himself.

"Now? Do we go plant them?" Aaron asked hopefully. Planting strawberries was hard work. You had to plant each one individually and water it. And yet, it seemed Aaron was looking forward to the task.

"I hope we plant them all," she mused, almost to herself.

"I'll plant them and then you can start watering the youngest rows," Aaron offered as he picked up two trays.

Lavina wasn't used to someone else helping and was about to offer to carry the trays for him. Luckily, she realized just in time that Aaron wasn't there for her company, he was there to work—so she might as well let him work.

Chapter 6
A Strange Feeling

Aaron hadn't been certain that moving into a barn and working for two Amish women was the right choice, but after only a week on the farm, he realized it was the perfect choice.

He had worked as a seasonal hand for the last five years and not once had he felt he was making such a big difference. Usually he worked in a team, only aiding in the eventual result of the harvest. But here, on the Gerber farm, he could see the difference he was making every day.

Where there had been empty row upon empty row of fertile soil just waiting to be planted, there were now hundreds of strawberry seedlings soaking up the sun as their roots strengthened to produce generous fruits in the future.

Aside from enjoying the work and the satisfaction he derived from it, Aaron was enjoying the Amish lifestyle. Without electricity to charge his phone, or being able to check emails or receive phone calls, it was as if time had slowed its pace. Instead, he could take time to enjoy the sunrise, instead of being hunched over a phone.

In the evenings, he thought about his religion, something he hadn't thought about for a long time. But witnessing the way Lavina and Miriam lived by their faith had inspired him to question his own.

He had never been a practicing member of the church. For his parents, belonging to a faith meant they had somewhere to go for baptisms, weddings and funerals. Unlike the Amish women, he had come to know over the last week.

On Sunday, regardless of Miriam's broken leg, or that Lavina had worked her fingers to the bone the entire week, they had set off for Sunday service in the buggy. When they returned, they looked refreshed and peaceful, something Aaron couldn't ever remember feeling himself.

Sunday lunch had been a generous meal with roasted potatoes, beef, vegetables, and with no one discussing calories or the latest series on Netflix. Instead, they had discussed the deacon's service from that morning.

Aaron found himself intrigued by their views of the world and how every decision, conversation, and day had their faith intertwined.

More than anything, Lavina intrigued him.

Aaron knew that as an outsider, a seasonal farmhand and a man that didn't know what he wanted from his future—it was ludicrous to be attracted to her. But it simply couldn't be helped. Not only did he find Lavina attractive in every sense of the word, he found her refreshing. She wasn't constantly fussing with her hair or running to touch up her makeup. She wore the same plain dresses every day with sensible shoes. Her hair was always braided beneath what he learned was a prayer kapp, and her smile was always easy.

In the past, Aaron had found attraction strike whenever he met a high maintenance girl with luscious curves and painted lips. The complete opposite of who and what Lavina was.

Lavina was hardworking, honest, loyal, and more than anything, she was kind.

Aaron had worked for many people in the past. Some farmers would simply chase you off their property if you did something wrong, others would berate you with loud voices and fisted hands.

But Lavina did neither. When he made a mistake, she would patiently demonstrate again and again. She would explain to him why the methods she used were so important and took the time to explain everything to him from root growth and fruit production.

Then there was Miriam.

Aaron's parents didn't have an active relationship with his grandparents when they had still been alive. Aaron remembered visiting them on the holidays and even then, the conversations would be terse and usually about investments, upcoming plans and what the latest market values were on their properties.

For Aaron, even as a teenager, it had felt more like a stock market meeting that it did a family visit.

But Lavina reminded him of what every mother or grandmother should be like. She was kind and gentle and made him feel welcome in her home. He couldn't once remember working as a seasonal hand and dining in the main house.

But Miriam insisted he take their meals with them.

Every meal time was an experience. The bond between Miriam and Lavina was clear in their every interaction. Once or twice, Aaron had wondered what it would feel like to have a bond like that with someone.

He certainly didn't have it with his parents.

"Aaron, is something wrong? You seem distracted?" Lavina asked, passing him the bowl of mashed potatoes.

Aaron smiled at Lavina's concern. "Nothing's wrong. I was just thinking about how much I enjoy Miriam's cooking."

Miriam laughed. "You better. Right now, it's the only thing I'm allowed to do."

"It's not the only thing," Lavina argued playfully. "You're allowed to do the dishes as well, as long as you don't carry anything."

"I think I miss that the most. I never realized how much time I spent carrying things. A cup of tea, a few potatoes, a pail of water… I hate having to ask you to help me the whole time," Miriam sighed.

Lavina shook her head. "You've helped me much more than I'm helping you now. Besides, I don't mind."

"How's the strawberries coming along?" Miriam asked before taking a bite of her beef.

Lavina glanced at Aaron with a secretive smile that made blood rush to his head. He swallowed past the excited lump in his throat. Lavina turned to Miriam, beaming from ear to ear. "It was a record planting. Every single seedling is in the ground. We lost a few because of the strong winds a couple of days ago, but the others will soon make up for it once they creep."

Miriam frowned and glanced at Aaron with a questioning look. "All the seedlings in the hayloft have been planted?"

"Yes ma'am," Aaron nodded.

Miriam laughed and shook her head in amazement. "Usually it takes Lavina and I about three weeks. How on earth did you do it so fast?"

Aaron shrugged. "You pay me to work, not to waste time. Besides, I'm having a hard time keeping up with Lavina. She's like a force of nature with planting."

"She is," Miriam agreed. "Luckily, I have age as an excuse to fall behind, what's yours?"

Aaron glanced at Lavina and smiled. His excuse would be her beauty distracting him, but it wasn't the place or the time, so instead he shrugged. "Her super humanly powers."

"Strength comes from Gott, and I pray for a little more every night," Lavina smiled easily.

There it was again, Aaron thought to himself. He glanced at Lavina before he turned to Miriam. He'd never known what he was searching for, but somehow sitting at the table with Lavina and Miriam made him feel as if he had found it.

He couldn't put a name to it or even pinpoint exactly what it was. But the hollowness in his chest seemed to fade.

Perhaps he had finally found what he was looking for.

The thought made him sad, because he only had to look at their clothes to know that this was only temporary. As soon as the season was over, he would return to his Englisch life and to them he'll just be the seasonal worker that came to help out.

But until then, Aaron planned on being the best seasonal worker they could've imagined hiring.

Chapter 7
Strawberry Field Confessions

Lavina had been against hiring the Englischer as their seasonal farm hand. When Miriam had made the split-second decision without even asking her opinion, she had believed it would take her a week to prove Miriam wrong.

But now, two weeks later, she knew she was going to have a hard time with it.

In fact, she wasn't even sure she wanted to prove Miriam wrong anymore, instead Miriam had proved her wrong.

Aaron was hardworking and hardly ever complained. Regardless of the fact that he lived in the barn, had no access to electricity, and worked for minimum wage, he seemed perfectly satisfied with the work and wage.

It made little sense to Lavina at all.

Although she could see Aaron had callouses from working hard, there was something about him, almost an air of stature or importance. She wasn't sure which. It was not that he gave her the impression that he was *more* than them. It was simply the way he did certain things. Like the way he ate, carefully cutting each piece of meat into a bite size before taking a bite. The way he served tea, as if he'd never held a teapot before.

Small things that made her curious about the man helping her make the best of the strawberry season were raising questions in her mind.

Who was Aaron really?

The biggest part of her curiosity was the way she felt when she was with him. He could make her laugh on a whim, treat her like a lady when he took the heavier load—something no one else has ever done for.

Lavina was perfectly comfortable with her age and her life, but she had never been treated as fragile or precious, something Aaron seemed to do daily.

She had scoured her bible for words of wisdom, but nothing seemed to ease her discomfort at the attraction she felt for him. Lavina knew very well after two weeks that she didn't merely like Aaron as a worker, she liked him.

She enjoyed working with him, spending time in his company and, more than anything, she enjoyed listening to his adventures of working on farms all across the country.

The attraction she felt for him couldn't lead to anything, and yet it seemed to grow a little more every day. Until now, she had made certain that neither Miriam nor Aaron noticed it, but Lavina wondered how much longer she could hide the unwanted feelings she was developing for a perfect stranger.

"You missed one," Aaron called out from his row.

Lavina glanced down at her feet and indeed he was right. She had been so deep in thought she had missed watering a seedling.

Now that all the seedlings were in, they were hand watered once a day, until the summer rain would drench the soil. It was a laborious task that took both her and Aaron most of the day. Walking back and forth to the water pump and watering each plant with just enough water to satisfy its thirst without drenching it.

"Denke," Lavina smiled at him and dipped her small tin into the water bucket before she watered the next one.

"Can I ask you something?" Aaron asked as he drizzled a few drops on one plant in his row.

The sun was shining hot on her back, the cool breeze easing the heat as she turned to Aaron. "Of course."

Lavina wasn't sure what Aaron wanted to ask, but he set down his water pail and turned to her with a questioning look. "How old were you when you came to live with Miriam?"

"Six years old. I still remember it was just a few weeks after my birthday. The only thing that survived the fire was my doll." Lavina sighed at the memory. The faceless doll had been a gift from her parents and still lay on her bed as a daily reminder of how quickly someone could be called home.

"And the fire... your parents... did they suffer?" Aaron asked carefully.

Lavina had thought about that many times over the years, but in her heart, she believed her parents didn't suffer. The explosion hopefully took them without pain. "I'm not sure, but I believe that the propane explosion would've eased their suffering. But I know that they don't have any cares, ailments or pain where they are now."

Lavina smiled up at the sun. Since she was a child, she imagined the heat from the sun was her parents' love shining down on her.

"You seem… so at peace with it," Aaron commented curiously.

Lavina shrugged. "Why wouldn't I be? We can't fight death and we can't blame Gott for calling someone home. Besides, calling my parents home gave Miriam the dochder she never had and me a chance of having another mamm. I think it worked out well."

"It did." Aaron smiled. "You belong together. I'm not even that close with my own parents."

"You're not?" Lavina asked, surprised. She couldn't imagine someone not having such a close bond with a parent or a guardian.

"Nope. Ever since I can remember, the nanny took care of me. When I got older, did it myself. They were there, but usually distracted or tired—they had little time to take care of me themselves." Aaron sounded bitter and hurt by the admission.

Lavina's heart clenched in her chest for how Aaron must have felt as a young boy who was cared for by the staff instead of his parents. "It sounds like they were busy."

"Yeah. Mom's a doc and Dad's a lawyer. Both demanding careers. Now they can't understand why I don't want to follow in their footsteps." Aaron sighed and shook his head. "It's because they don't know any different."

Lavina could hear the doubt and uncertainty in his voice. Wanting to ask a question of her own, she searched his gaze. "What do you want?"

Aaron chuckled and shook his head. "I've been trying to figure that out for the last five years. I thought if I got away from them and spent some time on my own, I would figure it out. But here I am and still no closer to choosing a career path or having any thoughts about returning home to Boston." Aaron sighed and turned to Lavina with an honest look. The honesty in his gaze made her feel special, that he had the courage to share his thoughts with her.

"It's just that… I don't want that life. I don't want to do stock analysis over Christmas, or see my family only when I'm tired and agitated. If I have a family, I want to enjoy them. I want to spend my days with them, like you and Miriam. I want a life that matters, that is full—not just financially viable. That is something my parents don't understand. It's like they don't understand me."

"Why would you say that?" Lavina asked carefully.

"Because that's how I feel. I think… as I child I felt in the way and now that I've grown up, I guess I feel like that isn't where I belong. One day, I'll look at a place or do a job and I'll know. I'll know I found the life I've been searching for," Aaron finished with hope shining in his gaze.

Lavina smiled with a nod. "That sounds like something to look forward to. You should ask Gott to lead you there."

"God? How can he help?" Aaron asked, looking baffled.

Lavina wasn't offended. She knew that not everyone practiced their religion as faithfully as the Amish. "Gott had a plan for your life since the day of your birth, Aaron. Instead of fumbling around on your own, and reaching into the dark, ask Gott to guide you to where you belong. If you have faith, you'll find it."

Aaron looked at her as if she had just spoken to him in Finnish. Lavina smiled, knowing that he might not understand what she meant now, but in time Gott would help him understand.

"I uhm… so you just ask him things like that?" Aaron asked, a little uncertainly.

This time Lavina couldn't help but laugh softly. "Aaron, he is our father in heaven. He is the reason for our presence on earth. He is everything. If we can't turn to him when we're in doubt, to whom must we turn? I ask him things every day. I say denke every day for my blessings. Sometimes I'll ask him for strength, other times I'll thank him for it. I can't imagine my life without talking to him…" Lavina mused, almost to herself.

A life without faith sounded terribly empty.

Aaron's eyes met hers and Lavina felt that familiar attraction pulse through her veins. When his smile curved, her heart skipped a beat. "Lavina Bowman, I think I can learn a lot more from you than just about farming strawberries."

Lavina returned the smile and knew that if she allowed herself, she could learn a lot from Aaron about love.

But she wouldn't allow herself to even consider the possibility.

Chapter 8
A Mother's Concern

While Aaron and Lavina stood in the field talking about faith, family, and the future, neither of them were aware of Miriam watching them from the living room.

Her broken leg was no longer causing her pain, but it was causing her much discomfort. The endless urge to scratch beneath the cast had caused her to always carry a knitting pin with her for when the itching became unbearable.

But right now Miriam wasn't concerned with her leg or the underlying itch, instead, she was transfixed by the interaction happening outside.

Ever since Lavina had been baptized two years ago, Miriam had encouraged her to go to Sunday singings. But Lavina showed no interest in thinking of her own future. Miriam loved that the girl she loved as if she were her own blood was independent, but she feared that Lavina was too independent.

Miriam's choice not to marry or have children stemmed from medical complications when she was a teenager.

Knowing that she could never bear children, Miriam had shied away from courtship. She didn't want a man to fall in love with her and promise that it won't matter, only to look at her with regret in the future. Miriam sometimes wondered if she had made the right decision, but she only had to look at Lavina to know that it blessed her with more than enough love.

But Lavina didn't have complications holding her back. Only the fear of leaving Miriam behind.

Although she had never once voiced that fear, Miriam knew Lavina like the back of her hand. She knew Lavina guarded her heart because she couldn't stand the thought of living a life of her own and leaving Miriam to grow old and lonely when the time came.

Now, as she watched Lavina laughing with Aaron in the fields, she witnessed something she had never witnessed before. Lavina enjoying a man's company.

Although the man was Englisch and hired on as a seasonal worker, it gave Miriam hope.

Perhaps Aaron had been sent here to open Lavina's eyes to the possibilities of what a relationship could hold for her. Perhaps it would make her more accepting of the thought of courtship and less hesitant to dream dreams of her own.

Miriam knew that when the time came for Lavina to marry, she wouldn't be able to keep the farm. But she had already accepted that in that event, she would sell off the farmland and keep the house. She wouldn't hold Lavina back with her own dreams.

Just like the old saying about setting a bird free, Miriam knew Lavina needed to use her wings and dreaming her own dreams. Lavina had suffered so much, so young in her life, the loss that no one should ever have to experience, and yet she didn't live with blame or anger.

She had a good heart, a kind disposition, and loyalty, such as Miriam had never encountered before. In her eyes, Lavina would make the perfect wife and mother, if only she could find a man to appreciate her for who she was.

Miriam leaned back on the sofa and closed her eyes before she prayed. Prayer could heal all concerns and ease all worries.

Gott, denke for blessing us with Aaron's presence. Denke for sending us someone of gut nature with a hardworking disposition. Bless him Gott and the journeys he will undertake when he leaves our farm. Gott, I want to ask that you touch Lavina's heart. Help her let go of the defenses and allow her to let in love. Help her to dream her own dreams, give her the courage to build her own future. Bless her with a mann that is as kind as he is generous. A mann that will treat her as his equal in decisions, but will treat her with love in their relationship. One that will be hardworking, one that will provide for her. Gott, I ask you this not because I fear you don't have a wonderful future in mind for Lavina, but because I want you to bless this mann as well. Help him notice Lavina and open his heart to your voice when the time comes, Gott. Amen.

Miriam opened her eyes and couldn't help but smile when she saw Aaron and Lavina splashing each other with water. She couldn't remember the last time she had seen Lavina play instead of work. The downside of living with an older woman for a companion meant Lavina had little opportunity to play.

Not for the first time, Miriam knew she had made the right decision by hiring Aaron. He was proving to be an asset for the season and he was proving to bring out the best in Lavina.

Miriam knew everything happened by Gott's hand, and she knew without a single doubt in her mind that Aaron's presence on her farm was Gott's work as well.

Perhaps Aaron needed to play just as much as Lavina.

Chapter 9
A Secret No One Knows

That evening Aaron found sleep hard to come by.

He thought back to his last days in Boston, and the reason he really left.

For the last five years, he'd convinced his parents and anyone who had asked that he left to find himself, to see the country, to live a little before he settled down with a career and a family.

But deep down, only Aaron knew those were lies.

No one knew the true reason he had left.

There had been no one at home that day and Aaron had left everything as he had found it, to avoid his parents knowing that he had discovered their biggest secret.

A secret that had changed everything for Aaron.

If only he hadn't gone looking for his birth certificate, he never would've found out.

He never would've learned that he wasn't actually a Richards. Instead, Richards was the adopted surname his parents gave him after they adopted him as a baby.

Until that moment, it had perfectly satisfied Aaron with going to college and leading the life his parents expected him to. But when his eyes had fallen on the adoption papers, everything inside him shifted.

Suddenly it made sense why he didn't look like his parents, why he didn't act like them and most of all, why he never felt as if he fit in with them. His whole life he had felt like an outsider and that day it had finally made sense why.

Because he never was one of them.

They had loved him as if he were their actual son, and Aaron knew if he revealed how he felt to his parents, they would've been shattered. So he had kept his silence and instead, found a reason to leave.

That very first year on the road, he had done everything within his power to find out who his real parents were. But dead end after dead end had him losing hope.

Not knowing how to return to Boston and pretend like he didn't know, he had stayed on the road. He had worked on farm after farm, learned trade after trade, trying to figure out how he could start a future if he knew nothing about his past.

The secret of his adoption had haunted him, had plagued his conversations with his parents, because he didn't know how to tell them he knew.

It was last year when he had finally had a breakthrough.

He could still remember calling social services again, like he had done so many times in the past, and asking them if they could unseal his adoption records. The lady had been reticent like all her colleagues before, but had promised to get back to him.

A month later, she had finally returned his call. The only information she had of any value was that his birth mother came from Pennsylvania. She had named a town that had meant nothing to Aaron back then, but this morning he had realized that Zook's Corner was the town the social worker had mentioned.

She couldn't unseal the records of give him the name of his birth mother, but she said that his mother had been Dutch.

As he stared up to the roof of the hayloft, Aaron frowned as the pieces fell into place. If his mother was from Pennsylvania, from right here in Zook's Corner, then she might not have been Dutch per se, but Amish.

It was as if a light had just flashed on in Aaron's mind.

He had given up on finding his birth mother and, without even realizing it; he had ended up in the very town where she had come from. And now he was working on an Amish farm.

For the first time in his life, Aaron couldn't help but believe that there was a greater power at play. He had always believed that destiny and fate were something that you held control over, and now he realized he didn't just happen to find a job in Zook's Corner.

Perhaps it had been subconscious, perhaps it was fate, perhaps it might just have been coincidence.

Either way, now that he was here, Aaron had renewed hope of finding his birth mother. He had given up the search more than a year ago, but now he was right in the town where his mother had lived back then.

Perhaps someone would remember, perhaps someone would know...

Or maybe he should just phone the social worker again and complete the official request for the files to be unsealed. It was a lengthy process, but perhaps it could work.

He didn't know how he could find a woman that had given a son up for adoption over twenty-three years ago, especially since he didn't have her name, but he had hope.

Aaron climbed out of bed and kneeled beside it. He remembered Lavina's explanation about how she consulted God on every matter in her life and for the first time, Aaron gave a matter over to God.

"Hi, I uh… I haven't really done this before, so I'm not sure how it's done. I guess, if I do what Lavina told me, it's just like having a conversation with a friend or a father. So, I'm Aaron Richards, but I guess you knew that. Since you're God and everything… I have something on my mind that's been troubling me for some time, but I guess you know that, too. I'm sorry, I'm fumbling through this a bit. I guess what I'm trying to say is that if you're really there, and you can really hear me, will you help me find them? My birth parents, I mean. I don't know why they can't just tell me who they are, but some red tape is stopping them from giving me more details. But apparently you cut through red tape.

Will you help me cut through the red tape of it all and find out who my real parents are? I don't want to hurt my parents, but I want to know. I want to know why I don't feel like I belong with them. I want to learn about my heritage, my past, my real family.

Well, that's all for now. But thanks, anyway.

Bye. I mean… Amen."

Aaron let out a heavy sigh. He wasn't sure how to pray, but he had a feeling he had just made a big mess of it. Hopefully, God would understand. He climbed into bed and wondered if his prayers would work. He wasn't sure anything would come of it. In fact, he doubted it very much, but he had to at least try.

Perhaps when he found his birth mother, he wouldn't feel like a feather drifting in the wind from town to town. Perhaps then he could finally begin living his own life instead of thinking about his past.

Chapter 10
Troubling Thoughts

Lavina wasn't one to pry, but it was hard not to when she could clearly see that Aaron had something on his mind when he returned from town.

Usually, Miriam did the marketing on Mondays, but this morning at breakfast, Aaron had offered to do it instead. Ever since he had returned from town, he seemed more than a little distracted.

Lavina couldn't help but fear that his distraction was actually disinterest. She knew that strawberry farming wasn't interesting for everyone and the last thing she needed now was for Aaron to leave before the harvest was over. He'd been such a great help over the last few weeks that she couldn't imagine getting everything done without him.

As they worked side by side through lunch into the afternoon, her concerns became more and more prominent, fearing that when he finally broke his silence, it would be to resign.

She left Aaron in the fields to get them some cold water from the house, since the sun was bearing down on them.

"Here you go," Lavina said, handing him a jug on her return. "It's hot today."

Aaron nodded without actually answering.

Not being able to keep her silence any longer, Lavina finally let out a heavy sigh. "Look, I can see something is the matter. If it's the work and you'd rather leave…"

Aaron's gaze shot up to meet hers. "What?"

Lavina's heart skipped a beat. Why was it that when he looked at her like that, it seemed the entire world simply disappeared? "I can see you have something on your mind. If you found another job, or you simply don't want to work here anymore, please don't feel obligated to stay."

The words hurt her almost as much as they tasted bitter on her tongue. She needed his help and would love to obligate him to stay, but she wouldn't if he wanted to leave. The most concerning thought for Lavina was how much she had come to care for Aaron over the last few weeks.

He was a hard worker and a good man and although he was Englisch, Lavina found the attraction between them hard to deny.

"Why would you think I found another job?" Aaron asked, clearly confused as he wiped the sweat from his brow.

Lavina shrugged. "You haven't said a word all morning."

Lavina could see confusion and indecision in his eyes before he shook his head. "I'm not leaving, I'm not resigning, and I haven't found another job…" Aaron trailed off.

Lavina frowned, feeling foolish and curious at the same time. "Is something wrong, Aaron? Is there something I can help with?"

"No, but thank you," Aaron answered quickly. "It's… it's a personal matter. And before you feel offended that I'm not telling you what it is, please don't. I've told no one before and I'm just having a little trouble dealing with it at the moment."

Lavina searched his gaze and could see that whatever was troubling him was weighing heavily on his mind. Her gaze softened and her words were kind when she finally spoke. "Then I'll keep you in my prayers. I'll pray that you get the strength and the courage you need to deal with it."

Aaron's smile softened. "One day, Lavina, one day when I'm ready to share it, you'll be the first person to know."

Lavina's smile widened. "Denke, your trust in me flatters me."

"Can I continue by flattering your strawberries? I snuck one while you went back to the house. They're delicious. I don't think I've ever tasted strawberries this good before," Aaron said, picking one off the vine and handing it to her.

Lavina bit into the sweet juicy fruit, the sting of sour hitting her tongue only for a moment before the sweetness took over. The grainy texture of the strawberry made her smile. "You're right, they are really gut."

Aaron let out a sigh of contentment as his gaze drifted over the strawberry fields. Lavina was used to the scent of strawberries in the air when the sun baked them ripe from above. It was a miracle she witnessed year after year, but she felt privileged to see that miracle through Aaron's gaze.

He appreciated it just as much as they did.

"Beautiful, isn't it?" Lavina asked, following his gaze.

Aaron turned and looked right at her. She could feel a blush rise in her cheeks as he held her gaze. "The most beautiful sight I've ever seen."

Lavina's heart swelled in her chest. She knew she was playing with fire, but she couldn't seem to stop herself. She had met no one like Aaron before and couldn't help but feel privileged to have him look at her like he was looking at her now.

When he looked away, the shadows quickly returned to his gaze.

Lavina wished he would tell her what was troubling him, but she did as she promised. She prayed for him.

When they continued working, it was once again with the rhythm of two people who had been working together for years. They moved swiftly as they harvested the ripe fruit, giving the plant a chance to push more nutrients into the younger fruit. It was a labor-intensive job, one that required many hours on your haunches, with the back on your sun, but Lavina didn't mind.

Because when they were done, they would have boxes and boxes of strawberries that farm stalls from all over the county would buy from them.

"That's it," Aaron announced when they reached the last row.

Lavina laughed. "That might be it for the strawberries, but we still have to feed the animals and stable the horses. I wonder what Miriam cooked for dinner?"

"She asked me to bring meatloaf ingredients from town, so I think that's what we're having," Aaron said as they began making their way back to the barn.

Lavina smiled with excitement. "No one makes meatloaf like Miriam. I don't know what she puts in it, but it's heavenly. The flavor is really magnificent. Did she ask you to bring ice-cream?"

Aaron nodded. "Yes, why?"

Lavina laughed. "Then you'd better wash some strawberries and bring them up to the house. Because tonight we're dining like kings."

Aaron smiled with a nod. "Strawberries and Ice-cream, fare fit for a king indeed."

"Exactly."

They finished the last of the chores and headed up to the house for dinner, but all the while Lavina could sense that Aaron still had a lot on his mind.

Deep down, she couldn't help but feel a little concerned for the secret he was keeping from her, but she didn't want to pry. She only hoped that Aaron's secret wouldn't bring trouble to their door.

As they sat down for meatloaf, vegetables, and fried potatoes, Lavina quietly said her prayers, once again including Aaron.

She couldn't help but feel concerned about him. Ever since he had worked on the farm, she had never seen him look this down or sad before. She wouldn't try guessing what was bothering him, but deep down, she couldn't help but wonder if it was family.

Although she only had Miriam now, Lavina couldn't imagine that it would be easy for Aaron to be away from his family for such a long time.

Perhaps that was what was troubling him. Perhaps it was time for him to go home and he wasn't ready to tell Miriam that.

A sigh escaped her as Miriam sliced into the meatloaf. "I hope this meatloaf turns those frowns upside down because there are strawberries and ice-cream for dessert."

Chapter 11
Fear of Falling

"Did you and Aaron have an argument?" Miriam asked as soon as Aaron's footsteps faded into the distance.

Lavina turned from the sink where she was washing the dishes, a frown already creasing her brow. "Nee, not at all."

"Then I wonder what is bugging him," Miriam said with a shrug.

Lavina sighed. "He's been like that all day. When I asked him about it, he said it was a personal matter."

"Ach nee, I hope he doesn't have to leave," Miriam's voice was filled with anguish.

"I asked him," Lavina revealed. "I was afraid that was why he was so... off."

Miriam frowned at Lavina and shook her head. "You seem awfully comfortable with him. Asking him such personal questions. A girl should never be too outspoken, Lavina."

Lavina set down the dish cloth after drying the last plate. "I wasn't being outspoken; I was simply concerned. He really seemed troubled, and I wanted to help."

If Miriam's frown had showed that she was concerned about how outspoken Lavina had been, the cocked brow she now summoned clearly indicated that she was a little disturbed by Lavina's concern. "Lavina...."

Lavina recognized the tone of voice and knew that it couldn't lead anywhere she wanted to go. "Don't look at me like that."

"Lavina, he's a seasonal worker. He'll be leaving when the season is over. I know I've encouraged you to open your heart, but an Englischer… ach nee Lavina, you know better," Miriam cautioned kindly.

Lavina refused to reveal her true feelings to Miriam. Although she loved her like a mother, she wouldn't admit out loud that somehow, she cared for the Englischer that lived in their hayloft. "I haven't opened my heart, Miriam. You're concerned about nothing, I assure you. It's merely a matter of Aaron being a big help on the farm. Tasks that took you and I two days to complete are now completed in a matter of hours. He's a hard worker and a fast worker at that. I'm merely concerned about losing the help before you're back on your leg."

Miriam huffed. "Today I made meatloaf and served dessert. I'd say I'm back on my leg again."

Lavina chuckled. "You're on your crutches. I can hardly see you struggling through the fields on a pair of crutches. Heaven help us if you break another leg, or your neck this time."

"My neck is perfectly fine, denke," Miriam teased back. "Lavina, why haven't you attended Sunday singings? All of your friends are attending and yet, Sunday after Sunday, you stay home and keep me company..." Miriam trailed off.

Lavina poured them each a cup of tea and joined Miriam at the table. "I just don't feel ready, that's all."

"Lavina, you're never ready for love until it knocks your feet from right out under you," Miriam said the words as if she had experience in that field, although Lavina knew she had never courted or wed.

"In that case, I'll keep crutches close by, because I don't intend to fall for someone… ever." The words she spoke were as much for her own assurance as for Miriam.

Not that Lavina didn't want a family of her own. It was simply a matter of being terrified at the thought.

"Why not? Falling in love is one of the most precious experiences you can have," Miriam explained.

Lavina frowned. "If it's so precious, why haven't you done it?"

"Just because I'm not married, and I had no kinner of my own, doesn't mean I never fell in love, Lavina," Miriam stated firmly.

"You… you had a beau?" Lavina asked, intrigued. She knew everything about Miriam, but she didn't know about this. "I thought you didn't court because of your… condition."

"I didn't court," Miriam agreed. "But I fell in love. It happened so fast I didn't even know it was happening until I found myself head over heels."

"Then what happened? Who was he? Where is he?" Lavina asked, curious to learn more about this side of Miriam she had never heard about.

Miriam took a sip of her tea and shrugged. "His name was Lucas, and it was a long time ago. I do not know where he is now. You still haven't told me why you refuse to fall in love."

Since Miriam had just shared an intimate secret with Lavina, she knew it was her turn. "Because... Before I explain, I want you to know that I love you like you're my very own mamm. And I only tell you this because you asked..."

"I'm listening," Miriam said easily, patiently waiting for Lavina to continue.

"That night... the night of the fire... I was so small, but I remember my chest hurting. I remember how much it ached to take a single breath. I remember crying myself to sleep. I remember standing at the grave of my parents, knowing I'd never see them again. I don't think I was old enough to understand everything, but I was old enough to know they weren't coming back. Later... as I got older, I dreamed of their bodies decomposing. I woke up with the same ache in my chest, the same pain that stabbed with every breath.... It's not that I don't want to fall in love and have a familye Miriam. It's that I can't stand the thought of losing another person who I love."

"Ach my dear Lavina," Miriam said, reaching for Lavina's hand across the table. "I never knew that's how you felt. If I'd have known, I would've told you this long ago."

"Tell me what?"

"I would've told you that a heart isn't an island. It needs the ocean to lap at its shores, it needs the trees to whistle in the wind. Alone, it's nothing but a heap of sand. Allow yourself to love Lavina, or your kindness, love, and generosity won't be any more than a sand bank jutting out of the ocean."

"I'm fine with having a sand bank for a heart," Lavina said, trying to hide her fear. "Besides, a hurricane can't come and ruin it."

"But it also won't bring you any joy. Just promise me one thing… promise me that when the time comes and the right mann crosses your path, you'll let him in. You'll lower the defenses you've constructed around your heart and let him see the real you," Miriam all but begged.

Lavina didn't say it out loud, but without realizing it, that was what happened with Aaron. Somehow, her defenses had been weakened, and he'd manage to sneak inside.

Nothing good could come of the feelings she had for Aaron, but that didn't mean she didn't have them.

It also didn't mean that she could just forget about it altogether.

"When the right mann comes, I will," Lavina said, hoping that one day she'd meet an Amish man that made her feel as important and special as Aaron did.

But until then, she had something else she needed to add to her prayers.

She had to ask the Lord to remove Aaron from her thoughts and from her heart, because the feelings she had for him weren't only inappropriate, they could only lead to one thing…

Heartbreak…

Chapter 12
Name or Shame

"Is there a reason you deliver to this farm stall and not the others?" Aaron asked as he climbed into the buggy beside Lavina.

Lavina smiled fondly with a shrug. "Mr. Yoder was Miriam's first client when she started growing strawberries. Through the years, he's become her best. He has a standing order every season and when we have strawberries left after all the other farm stalls collect their orders, he always helps us out with buying those as well. Call it personal service for a good customer."

Aaron nodded. "How long has Miriam been growing strawberries?"

Lavina laughed and shook her head. "Ten years, this year. I still remember our very first harvest. I was eight years old and nearly ate the entire harvest by myself." Lavina turned to him with affection in her gaze. "Miriam didn't even scold me once. She just told me that strawberries were our future. Our future together."

"She sounds like a wonderful woman," Aaron commented as Lavina waved to Mr. Yoder on the porch of the farm stall, before calling to the horse to step-up.

"She is. She's the best," Lavina said without hesitation.

Aaron admired Lavina and Miriam's relationship, mostly because he didn't have such a close relationship with his own mother. Their relationship proved to Aaron that blood didn't always create the bond, but love did.

And yet, he still couldn't stop thinking about the social worker in Boston. He'd called her again a few days ago to find out if the records could be unsealed. After a detailed explanation of how a closed adoption works, Aaron had pleaded yet again.

Although he knew his parents loved him beyond measure, he wanted to know. It felt as if he was closer to finding his birth mother than he'd ever been before and yet, he had nothing to prove his gut feeling was right.

"She would've made a wunderbaar mamm," Lavina said almost to herself. "It's a shame Miriam couldn't have kinner of her own. That's why she never married."

Aaron frowned, feeling sympathy for Miriam. Lavina was right, Miriam would've made a wonderful mother. "So until she took you in, she had been alone?"

"Jah, and then it was just us two," Lavina agreed.

Aaron looked out towards the road leading to town. Lavina had a few chores to do in town, but he had one of his own. Aaron wanted to follow up with the social worker, although he knew it would be another wasted call.

For the first time, he realized that he wanted to share his secret with someone. He knew she wouldn't be able to help him, but just the thought of sharing this burden he'd been carrying for five years made him feel lighter already.

But even if he wanted to, what would he tell her? That he thought his mother lived in the community? That when he found her, he wanted to uproot her whole life by telling her he's the son she gave away?

Even if he learned who his true mother was, Aaron realized that confronting her wouldn't be that simple. If she was Amish, she would've had to have a good reason to give him up for adoption. He couldn't see Amish folks just giving away their babies.

It didn't matter how he thought about it, he realized that finding his birth mother could bring her trouble.

Was that really what he wanted?

"We have to stop by the grocer and the bakery. I'll do the grocery run, if you'd do the bakery run?" Lavina asked as she positioned the horse against the sidewalk where the buggy was perfectly parked.

"Sure, just tell me what you need," Aaron replied distractedly.

Lavina handed him a list and an envelope. "That should be enough. I'll meet you back here."

They each went their separate ways, but instead of going to the bakery, Aaron rushed to the nearest pay phone. He had to phone the social worker again.

He dialed the number he knew from memory and waited for her to answer. After explaining who he was, he could hear the recognition ring in her voice.

"Aaron, I've been trying to reach you all week. But your phone just says out of service?"

"Yeah, I'm having trouble with the signal where I'm staying at the moment," Aaron answered. "Why were you trying to reach me?"

"The judge refuses to unseal the records. It turns out your birth mother was a minor. But I found something that might be of help to you…"

Aaron's breath caught. Finally another bread crumb. "I'm listening."

"They gave her home address in the Amish community north of Zook's Corner, and I found something else… her last name. I know it's not much to go on, especially since most Amish folks share the same last name, but I thought…"

Aaron didn't wait for her to finish her trail of thought. "What's her last name?"

"Gerber…"

"Thanks," Aaron replied as his mind raced through a million thoughts at once. "I guess it would be foolish to ask if you could ask about unsealing those records again."

"No, I'm afraid it wouldn't help. These laws are there to protect the mother and the judge will not sway. Just… please don't tell anyone that I told you this. I could lose my job…"

Aaron nodded. "No one will ever know. Thank you so much."

Aaron ended the call and rushed to the bakery to get everything on Lavina's list.

Gerber

The name kept sounding over and over in his mind. The only Gerber he knew about in the community was Miriam.

Which made no sense at all? Miriam had never been married and couldn't have children. There was no way she could be his mother.

Perhaps there was another family member, a sister, a mother or even a cousin…

He met Lavina at the buggy and had to take a few deep breaths to calm himself before he turned to her with a serene smile.

"Does Miriam have any family in the community? Parents, siblings, cousins…"

Lavina laughed heartedly. "We're Amish. Most of us are cousins. But as for parents, she lost them years ago in a buggy accident. As far as I know, she's an only child. Why?"

Aaron shrugged. "Just wondering. I guess I just thought all Amish families are large."

Lavina cocked a brow. "Just like I thought all Englisch men were afraid of getting their hands dirty.

Their gazes met and Aaron felt that jolt of attraction again. He felt a connection with Lavina he couldn't explain. Almost as if his heart had become a magnet, and Lavina's smile a magnetic force.

He glanced away, trying to understand how his feelings for Lavina could be so strong. They lived in different worlds and yet he had never felt more at home that in their hayloft.

Aaron had spent the last five years trying to find answers and now that he was closer than ever before, he felt more confused than he'd felt in his entire life.

Chapter 13
Night Jaunts
& Nightmares

Aaron waited until he could see the house was completely dark.

He could hardly believe what he was about to do, but what he'd noticed over dinner had only assured him it was the only way to learn the truth.

After learning that his birth's mother's name was Gerber, he had been a little disappointed to learn Miriam had no other family by that name in the community. He had felt as if he would never learn the truth about his birth mother until he had sat down at the dinner table.

It was something simple, something he had never picked up on before, but it had struck him as a strange coincidence.

Ever since he could remember, Aaron had a mole on his right cheek. He'd thought nothing of it. But tonight, when Miriam had laughed at something Lavina had said, he noticed Miriam had the same mole.

At first, he had thought nothing of it, but then he noticed the shape of her lips and the color of her eyes.

Having one feature in common with another person might be coincidence, but to have the same mole, the same color eyes, the shape of mouth and to have the last name he was looking for…

It couldn't just be coincidence.

He knew Lavina swore Miriam couldn't bear children, but that didn't mean it had always been that way. Aaron felt guilty for doubting Lavina's words, but his need to learn the truth made him determined.

At first, he had considered waiting until morning to confront Miriam, but that idea had quickly evaporated when he realized how offensive that might be. Not only would he accuse her of abandoning her child, but he would also infer that she had been lying to Lavina all along.

The last thing Aaron wanted to do was to offend the two women that were not only given him a home but the trust of hiring him as their farm worker.

Instead, Aaron remembered about DNA testing. He had watched quite a few series about crime over the years, and could clearly remember that once DNA was discarded, you no longer needed permission to use it.

So if he was being honest, he thought, as he carefully made his way from the barn to the house, he would not steal anything, instead he was simply going to collect a piece of discarded DNA. It was the only way that he could find out whether Miriam was his mother without offending both her and Lavina.

They wouldn't even notice that he had taken something. He'd be as quiet as a mouse, and if the results came back inconclusive, no harm would be done.

Aaron quietly opened the back door and walked into the dark house. He had thought of either procuring a toothbrush, hair from a hairbrush, or to search through the burn bin for discarded nail clippings. But as he stood in the kitchen, guilt overwhelmed him.

Just standing in the kitchen without their knowledge was a betrayal of the trust, and Aaron hated knowing that he was about to deceive them even more. Instead of heading towards the bedrooms or the bathroom, he moved towards the living room.

On the couch where Miriam spent most of her time ever since she had broken her leg, there lay a prayer kapp. It was the perfect item to retrieve strands of Miriam's hair from, and to have them tested to see if her DNA matched his.

He picked it up and removed a few strands of hair before tucking them into a Ziploc bag he had brought along for that purpose. He counted ten strands of hair in total. Since he had never collected DNA samples before, he wasn't sure if it would be enough, but he hoped to at least rule Miriam out if not confirm if they were related.

Knowing that he had to do all of this before either Mariam or Lavina learned what he was up to, Aaron collected his phone, jacket, and wallet from the hayloft before he set off on the long walk to town.

He was grateful to find the diner still open and found a booth where he could charge his phone. He found the details of a DNA laboratory in Pennsylvania online, with a postal address on the website. Aaron got an envelope from the manager on duty and inserted both samples of his hair and Miriam's before addressing it to the laboratory.

He finished his coffee, switched off his phone, and dropped the envelope in the mailbox outside.

Aaron did not know how long the test would take, or when he would have the results, but at least he charge his phone enough to switch it on at least once a day and hope for a good enough signal to check his messages.

He walked back to the farm, arriving in the early hours of the morning, completely exhausted.

Aaron glanced at the house and noticed that Lavina's light had been switched on. She was already up, and he had yet to go to bed.

It would be another hour before they expected him for breakfast, and Aaron made the best of that time by catching a few winks of sleep.

Sleep dragged him under within minutes. His dreams were vivid and disconcerting as he found himself in a reality much different from the one that he was in.

In his dream he reunited with his mother. But his mother wasn't Miriam. It was a woman he had never seen before, with the same mole, the same color of eyes, and the same shape of mouth as his. Behind the woman stood Miriam and Lavina, looking at him with condemnation in their eyes. He had broken the trust and used them to serve his purpose. He had betrayed them.

In his dream he tried to explain to Lavina why he had done it, but Lavina simply shook her head, and said she should've never have trusted him.

Her words made his chest ache so badly that he could feel it even in sleep. If Aaron had ever wondered what a broken heart would feel like, he experienced it now. Although he knew that he and Lavina weren't compatible, that didn't mean he didn't love her.

Aaron had been so focused on trying to convince Lavina to forgive him that he didn't hear the words his birth mother spoke. Until the woman in his dream touched his arm and said it with such anger that it felt like a slap to his face.

"You don't belong here. You never belonged here. That's why I gave you away. You're not one of us."

Aaron shot up in bed, cold sweat beading on his forehead from the nightmare.

He knew it was only a dream, but the hatred and anger in the woman's gaze made a chill run down his spine.

He felt anxiety coil in his belly, wondering if that was truly the reason his mother had given him up. His throat closed up even as his hands shook.

Had he done the right thing last night, or only the right thing for himself?

It was too late now to stop the wheels he had put in motion, he realized with a heavy heart.

He wasn't sure what the results of the DNA test would be, but he knew he had just taken a step that could irrevocably change his future and his relationship with Lavina.

A sigh escaped him, knowing he was fooling himself.

He didn't have a relationship with Lavina, she was Amish and he was Englisch.

There would be nothing between them except for the working relationship of a farmer and a seasonal farm worker.

Chapter 14
An Appropriate Distance

"Lavina, I can't find my prayer kapp!" Miriam called from her bedroom.

Lavina chuckled to herself as she put the pot of coffee on the woodstove before making her way to the Livingroom. Usually, Miriam was very particular about putting her things back in their place, but ever since she had broken her leg, she had become a little forgetful.

Lavina didn't mind. She knew it was the pain medicine that made Miriam a little groggy. She also knew that the prayer kapp usually fell off in the living room if Miriam fell asleep on the couch.

She opened the curtains and let in the morning light before she searched the living room. "Did you put it in the laundry hamper?" There was no sign of the prayer kapp anywhere.

"Nee, I would've remembered. Ach... never mind, it will come out eventually," Miriam called back. "I swear it doesn't just feel like I've lost use of my leg. It feels like I'm losing my mind."

She leaned over the sofa and saw the prayer kapp had fallen off and was lying on the floor between the wall and the sofa. "Found it!"

After taking Miriam's prayer kapp to her, Lavina returned to the kitchen. Lavina finished making their coffee before she started on breakfast.

When Miriam joined her on her crutches, she couldn't help but sympathize. "You must be tired of those."

"Very. In fact, I despise them so much I've even named them. Judas and Judas's wife."

Lavina chuckled. "Maybe you should instead name them after the disciples. They are helping you."

"Don't remind me," Miriam let out with a sigh.

"Only a few more weeks to go," Lavina assured her, although she knew it would be much longer than that before Miriam would be back to her old self again.

"I've been thinking. I know we can't really afford it at the moment, but with the harvest looking as promising as it does, perhaps we should ask Aaron to stay on a little longer than just for the season? We could use a little more help around here," Miriam said, letting out a sigh of relief once she was seated at the table.

Lavina shrugged. "I'm not sure he'll be interested. He's still a little off."

"Well, we can ask. Where is he?" Miriam asked, glancing towards the barn. "Isn't he usually here by now?"

Lavina nodded as she placed two fried eggs onto a plate for Miriam. "Jah, he is. He must have overslept."

"This looks delicious. The perfect way to end a fast," Miriam smiled at the plate. "You always fry them just right. Mine always break."

Lavina joined her with a plate of her own. "You can make meatloaf, I can fry eggs. We all have our strengths."

"Just like your strength has always been bringing me joy," Miriam said fondly.

As they ate their breakfast, Lavina told Miriam about the strawberry fields and how the harvest was slowly beginning. Miriam listened eagerly, but Lavina didn't miss the fact that Miriam kept glancing towards the barn for when Aaron came to join them.

By the time Lavina had finished washing the dishes and settled Miriam in the living room, Aaron had yet to arrive. Since he skipped breakfast, Lavina packed him a small breakfast of a sandwich and an apple before she set off to start with the morning chores.

As soon as she stepped into the barn, she heard movement in the hayloft above.

"Guten mayrie. I brought you breakfast since you overslept," Lavina called out with a smile.

Personally, she detested it if she overslept. It just felt as if her whole day had started out wrong, but she also knew that leaving Miriam to sleep in did her the world of good sometimes. Hopefully, it had the same effect on Aaron, since his dour mood was worrying her.

"Thanks, I don't know what happened," Aaron said as he climbed down from the hayloft.

"It happens. Did you at least sleep well?" Lavina asked, turning to him. She had to consciously hide the surprise on her face. It didn't look as if Aaron had slept at all. Instead, he looked exhausted. There were dark circles around his eyes, his hair was tousled and even his clothes seemed rumpled.

"Fine, thanks," Aaron said as he accepted the sandwich and the apple. "Thanks for this too."

Lavina nodded, feeling very confused. "Aaron, I know you said it was a personal matter that has been bothering you, but are you sure you're all right?"

Aaron shrugged. "Yeah, I'll be fine." He glanced at the horses and turned to Lavina with a look of determination. "If you feed and water the horses, I'll get started on watering the strawberries."

"It's not watering day. We're harvesting today." Lavina couldn't help but find his confusion curious. Ever since he had begun working on the Gerber farm, Aaron had been the one to remember the schedule perfectly, even reminding Lavina of it once or twice.

He was completely out of sorts.

"I must still be fast asleep," Aaron laughed. "I'll do the horses and you look at which rows you want to be harvested today."

Lavina nodded with a curious frown. She did as he asked her to do, but as she made her way through the fields of strawberries, she couldn't help but feel as if something was amiss.

Aaron had been a little distracted over the last week, but today he simply seemed completely confused.

The barriers around her heart rose as quickly as they had fallen. Lavina wasn't someone to distrust people, but she felt as if Aaron was holding something back. She didn't know what it was, but it made her wonder if she should trust him as openly as she had done.

She couldn't let him go because she needed his help, but that didn't mean she couldn't close off her heart before she became even more involved that she already was.

Lavina glanced towards the barn as Aaron came walking towards her. He might be the only man that had ever made her heart swell with joy or her chest fill with love, but she would not let him in any further.

Right from the start she had known nothing could come of the attraction she felt towards Aaron. Now she realized that secretly she had been hopeful.

It was time for her to create the appropriate distance between her and Aaron.

The distance of an Englischer and an Amish.

The distance between an employer and an employee.

A distance that would protect her and give her enough space to realize that Aaron could be nothing more than he already was.

A seasonal worker that would leave and a man who had no future in her world.

Chapter 15
A Mailman Monday

"I'll take these to the buggy," Aaron said as he picked up a couple of boxes to deliver to Mr. Yoder.

Every day, their harvests were becoming a little bigger and more rewarding. The strawberry vines kept growing luscious fruits as the weather held, delivering glorious fruit.

Aaron had never seen strawberries as big or tasted strawberries as delicious as the ones he harvested on the Gerber farm.

He also hadn't expected to enjoy strawberry farming as much. The work was much more labor intensive than any other farm work he had done, and from the mind of an Englischer, he could see how modern technology could not only reduce the labor but increase the profits.

But he also learned in the month since his arrival on the Gerber farm that here everything wasn't about profit. It was about family, community, and God.

Unlike the world where he came from.

Aaron respected that Lavina and Miriam only planted enough vines that they could handle. They didn't plant more, and they didn't compromise on quality for quantity.

Instead, each strawberry vine was meticulously cared for. The strawberries were watered by hand instead of with a sprinkler system every second day and the large berries harvested on the days in between. Some days, they would harvest barely any strawberries at all and then suddenly they would harvest five to ten boxes a day.

Unlike the different sizes of strawberries you could find in the grocery stores back home, here Lavina only harvested the strawberries when they reached a certain size. She even had a couple of wooden pegs that she had marked for size that helped Aaron harvest the right ones.

They harvested just as they reached the perfect color and size, before the color darkened too much or the flavor was compromised by being on the vines too long.

It was an art.

It wasn't simply another method of farming, like all the ones he had learned about in the past.

It had been a little more than a week since he had snuck out in the middle of the night to send the DNA samples to the laboratory. Since he wasn't sure when they would have the results, he had asked them to mail it to the Gerber farm as soon as they had clarity on whether Miriam Gerber was his birth mother.

Aaron's gaze travelled towards the post box that stood on the edge of the property, wondering when the next mail delivery would arrive. He had been keeping a close eye on the mailbox, hoping to intercept when the mailman arrived.

"We can deliver them in the morning," Lavina said, interrupting his thoughts as she brought another four boxes to the buggy.

"Will Mr. Yoder be buying these?" Aaron asked curiously. It seemed like an awful lot of strawberries for just one farm stall.

"Jah. He gets out word to the community and his Englisch customers this time of year. He never has trouble selling them at all," Lavina explained.

"That's good. At least they won't go to waste," Aaron said as a frown creased his brow. He could see the mail van approach and felt his heart skip a beat.

Was today the day he learned about his family?

"I'll go fetch the mail," Aaron started towards the mailbox and arrived just as the van came to a stop.

The mailman climbed out and handed him two envelopes before he climbed in and continued with his deliveries.

Aaron glanced at the first envelope –addressed to Miriam. He tucked it into his pocket and saw his name on the second envelope.

For a moment, it felt as if his knees had simply vanished. He didn't have any feeling in his legs. They were completely numb, just like his hands that held the envelope.

The answer to his question, to his past, could be in the envelope, or it could just prove that his imagination was working.

"Letter from your familye?" Lavina asked, suddenly by his side.

Aaron cleared his throat and summoned a smile. "It seems that way. Would you mind if I take a few minutes to read it?"

Lavina nodded, but Aaron was already walking quickly towards the hayloft. He didn't feel Lavina's curious gaze on his back or even think about giving her the letter addressed to Miriam.

Aaron quickly climbed up the ladder and moved to the bed. He sat down and drew in a deep breath. *"I asked you to help me find answers…. Let's hope this is your way of helping."*

Aaron carefully sliced open the envelope, holding his breath the entire time. He wasn't sure what he wanted the news to be. If the test confirmed Miriam was his mother, it would mean that the search was finally over.

If it confirmed that she wasn't, Aaron would've spent another five weeks of his life trying to learn from the past.

The words swam on the page before his eyes. There were a few medical terms that he didn't wholly understand, but he understood the last sentence on the page.

For all the parties involved, this DDC DNA test was conducted according to state regulations. This test, conclusively confirms that Miriam Gerber is the maternal mother of one Aaron Richards. Although no DNA test can be 100% accurate, the results were 99.6% indicative of the maternity.

Aaron let go of his breath, struggling to realize what the words meant. He wasn't sure if he was more shocked that he found his birth mother through a seasonal worker advertisement, or that he had been living on her property for the last month.

Suddenly, all his conversations with Miriam flitted through his mind. The laughter, the kindness, the shared meals…

The lies about her not being able to have a child.

Was he the reason she had never married? Had she carried too much guilt about giving him up for adoption, that she never sought to have another child?

Questions swirled in his mind, and he couldn't find the answers to one of them.

Only the one he had been asking for the last five years.

Miriam Gerber was his birth mother, and right now, she was less than a hundred yards from his reach.

A heavy sigh escaped him as looked at the words on the letter again. The answer he had been searching for was finally within his reach and yet he felt the fear of rejection.

She had already rejected him on the day she had given him up for adoption.

Would she reject him again if he went to her now?

For a moment, Aaron felt like a little lost boy. On the one side, he had the parents that had raised him and loved him since he could remember. He had a childhood filled with love and memories of wonderful times they had shared.

And on the other, he had the papers he'd seen in his father's office.

The papers revealing that he was adopted.

He couldn't help but wish he'd never learned the truth.

But if he hadn't learned the truth, he would've continued a life that didn't feel like his.

Aaron said a prayer and drew strength and courage from it before he tucked the letter into his pocket and climbed down from the hayloft.

When he crossed the yard towards the house, he knew Miriam and Lavina would be gathered in the kitchen for lunch. Guilt overwhelmed him, knowing that he was about to ruin Miriam's day with the truth.

Hopefully Lavina could find it in her heart to forgive Miriam for the untruths she had been telling her for years.

Miriam could have children, and she did.

She had Aaron.

Chapter 16
Lunch Revelations

"Aaron, there you are. Did you receive news from your familye?" Lavina asked as soon as Aaron stepped into the kitchen.

Aaron shook his head and Lavina could instantly tell something was wrong. Whatever had been in the letter he had just received had upset him. For a moment, she couldn't help but care, but she reminded herself to keep her distance.

"Aaron, is something the matter? You're as pale as a sheet," Miriam said, noting the obvious. "Lavina, you shouldn't be working him this hard. He might not be used to being in the sun all day. The last thing we need is for him to get is sunstroke."

"It's not sunstroke," Aaron whispered. "Would you mind if I asked you something?"

Lavina glanced at Miriam, confused why he would ask her something about the farm and not Lavina.

"Jah, of course. Although with the strawberries, Lavina knows almost more than I do," Miriam said with a fond smile for Lavina.

Aaron shook his head. "It's not about the strawberries. His voice was crackling with nerves, as he cleared his throat. "It's about the son you gave up for adoption."

Lavina shook her head in a frown. "Aaron, you must be confused. Miriam can't have kinner. I've told you that...."

Lavina trailed off when she saw the ashen look on Miriam's face. Lavina watched as Miriam's eyes shone with tears before a smile slowly curved the corners of her mouth. It wasn't a cheerful smile; it was one of sadness and relief, almost.

She couldn't be sure what was happening, but it was as if she had disappeared to Miriam and Aaron as their gazes held. "What..." Lavina was about to ask when Miriam asked.

"It's you?" Miriam asked softly.

Aaron nodded, his features unreadable. "I received conclusive DNA test results today."

"My dear seeh," Miriam said before she stood up and began hopping on her crutches towards Aaron.

Lavina glanced at the two, completely baffled. Miriam couldn't have children. She had told Lavina so many times over the years, which made this situation even more unplausible.

Aaron stepped back, his face hard and cold. "So you can have children?"

"I could..." Miriam sighed. She hopped towards the table, the shock and gravity of the moment clearly making it hard for her to balance on the crutches.

"Sit down, Miriam, please. You look as if you're about to faint," Lavina said, taking control of a situation she didn't understand. "You too. If you want her to talk about whatever you know, you're sitting down. She can't very well hop after you," Lavina said firmly.

Aaron nodded and sat down at the table across from Miriam.

Knowing that the moment called for a strong cup of coffee, Lavina set about making it before she joined them.

"How did you find me?" Miriam asked, searching Aaron's eyes.

"I didn't," Aaron said simply. "I've been searching for years and only learned two weeks ago that my birth mother was from Zook's Corner and her surname was Gerber. Other than that, I couldn't learn anything else." Aaron pointed to the mole on his cheek. "You have one too."

Miriam nodded. "My daed had the same one."

Lavina stood up and fixed them each a cup of coffee, adding extra sugar for them all.

"Miriam, here. What is he talking about?" Lavina said, setting down Miriam's cup in front of her.

Miriam smiled up at Lavina with love and apology in her eyes. "I told you I couldn't have kinner. I never told you I had one…"

"Tell me now," Lavina joined them at the table.

"I was a young girl. I can still remember that summer as if it were yesterday. Some of my friends were going on an extended rumspringa and I… I wanted so much to go with. Not because I didn't want to join the church, but because I wanted to experience a little of the Englisch world before I did." Miriam sighed into her cup before she continued. "I found work as a waitress at a diner. At first it was just fun being able to wear Englisch clothes and spend my evenings listening to the other girls and the adventures they had. But then I met him… Joshua Lazenby."

"Is that my real father?" Aaron asked.

Miriam nodded. "He sat in my section one day and we talked. Before I knew it, he was coming in everyday just to see me. I fell in love with him so quickly... It was the first time in my life I considered leaving my heritage... my culture and my family behind. He was kind and generous and goodness... he was handsome–just like you are. I didn't see it before, but now... you take after him...."

"What happened?" Aaron asked impatiently.

Lavina wanted to tell him to give Miriam a moment, but she was just as curious to learn more about Joshua Lazenby.

"We began dating. I was going to spend six months in the city and I thought spending a few of those months with him wouldn't do any harm. I soon learned differently. I questioned everything about my life, because I wanted a life with him. I didn't want to be Englisch, but I wanted to be with Joshua. One weekend, he took me away to a cabin on a lake. He asked me then to leave the ordnung and become Englisch. He asked me to marry him." Miriam wiped away a tear.

"I was so overwhelmed with love for him I didn't hesitate. We spent a wonderful weekend at the lake... I loved him...," Miriam said with apology in her eyes.

"His parents, they were wealthy. Really wealthy. And he promised he would take care of me when I married him. But the next week, Joshua and his parents died in a plane accident. They were flying to the Hamptons to visit his family and something went wrong. I never saw him again... we hadn't even told anyone that we were engaged."

Lavina reached for Miriam's hand and gripped it. "I'm so sorry Miriam, you must've been heartbroken."

"I was," Miriam agreed with a sad smile before she turned to Aaron, "but I didn't yet know about the baby. We weren't taught about these things the Englisch girls are. I didn't even know I was with child until my mother realized it."

There was a silence that hung over the table, one that could be cut with a knife with anticipation.

"I returned home after I learned of Joshua's death. I wanted nothing more to do with the Englisch world. When I began to feel unwell, I thought it was just my grief. When my clothes fit poorly, I thought it was because I was eating too much, because I'd missed my mamm's cooking. And then... then my mamm told me she knew. At first, I didn't even know what she meant until she explained. They took me to the Englisch doctor the very next day. I was three months along..."

"And Joshua wasn't there to support you." Lavina's heart went out to Miriam. To have a child out of wedlock in an Amish community was a terrible sin. To have an Englishman's child... even worse.

"Nee. My mamm and daed were terribly ashamed and angry. They packed me up and sent me on a bus to Boston to stay with an aunt. I was told to stay there until I dealt with my problem and never to speak of it again." Miriam turned to Aaron. "I wanted to keep you so badly. You were all I had left of Joshua, but I knew my parents would never accept me. My aunt... a distant relative that had broken away from the church to become Englisch, kept telling me I couldn't care for you. I couldn't give you the life you deserved. The life your daed would've given you. She convinced me… she persuaded me that giving you up was the right thing to do."

"So you just signed me over…" Aaron asked bitterly.

Miriam laughed wryly. "You really think it was that easy? Jah, I signed a piece of paper, but they had to pry you from my arms. Once you were gone, they kept me sedated for three days because I wanted to find my seeh. It's because of the sedation that I didn't feel something was wrong. They only learned about the infection when it was too late… I had a hysterectomy four days after you were born. I lost not only my seeh that week, Aaron, I lost the possibility of ever having a family again."

Lavina glanced at Aaron and could see that there was sympathy in his eyes. She squeezed Miriam's hand and smiled at her with empathy. "You have me."

"And bless Gott for that. When he sent you to me… it was as if he had finally forgiven me for giving up my only child…." Miriam turned to Aaron. "But I have yet to forgive myself. Can you ever forgive me?"

Aaron wiped his eyes, which were damp with tears. "I never thought…. I just thought you didn't want me. I thought you just wanted to get rid of me… but now I realize that wasn't true. I can't imagine how hard it must have been for you."

"It is still hard. Every day I woke up thinking about you, every night I prayed for your wellbeing and now… here you are right before my very eyes…" Miriam's tears kept rolling over her cheeks.

"I didn't know I was adopted. My parents never told me. I only found out a few years ago. I've struggled all these years to get the documents unsealed. It was a closed adoption so they wouldn't tell me who my mother was." Aaron smiled. "Now I know it was you."

"Your parents…" Miriam trailed off. "Did they take gut care of you?"

"They gave me the life you wished I would have. A life of privilege and love."

Lavina knew it was only right to give Aaron and Miriam a little privacy. She also knew she needed a moment to herself to process what she had just learned.

Aaron was no longer just a seasonal farm worker living in their hayloft.

He was Miriam's only son.

Chapter 17
A Secret Worth Sharing

For the last week, Lavina had been concerned about Aaron. The more and more distant and worried he became, the more she wanted to create a barrier between her heart and the man that had stolen it.

She had been guessing for a week at what could be troubling him. First, she thought maybe his family wanted him to return home. Then she had thought maybe he received news that someone was ill. When that didn't suit, she guessed maybe he had lost someone close to him.

Last night, the most horrid of guesses had come to mind: that he had a girlfriend waiting for him back home.

But none of her guesses in her wildest dreams could've prepared her for what she had just learned.

Of course, she felt betrayed that Miriam had kept a secret like that all these years, but could she really blame her? Miriam had carried the burden of that secret her whole life and it wasn't Lavina's place to question Miriam about something that had happened before she had even come to live with her.

But now, after learning the truth, Lavina understood why Miriam had never fallen in love again. It had shattered her by the consequences of falling in love for the first time. Not only had she lost the sweetheart she had been ready to give up everything for, but her parents had forced her to give up her child, too.

She couldn't blame Miriam, not one bit, for keeping her secret so closely guarded.

And as for Aaron…

After working with Aaron for more than a month, Lavina knew Aaron wasn't a liar. He might have lied by omission, by not telling her about his search for his adopted mother, but he wouldn't lie to her and Miriam about this.

Could she be angry with him for coming to work for them?

Could she blame him for trying to find his birth mother?

Could she even harbor hatred because he had learned it was Miriam?

No, she couldn't.

And yet she felt as if she was the one that had been betrayed. She felt as if she was the one that couldn't come to terms with the revelations that had just taken place in the kitchen. For a moment, she wished Aaron had said nothing at all.

But she knew that the secret Aaron had held and the one Miriam had been carrying all these years were secrets worth sharing.

Lavina knew that only by learning the truth, it had set both of them free from the pain and the lies of their past.

She sank down on a bucket inside the barn, feeling overwhelmed.

Not knowing what else to do, she closed her eyes and prayed. *"Gott, please help me understand why I am feeling this way. I'm happy for Aaron that he finally found the birth mamm he has been searching for. I am relieved for Miriam that she doesn't have to carry the burden of her past anymore. I know I'm supposed to be happy for them and yet I feel anxious. I feel anxious and... concerned. Why now Gott? Why do you reveal all of this now, when Aaron is going to leave and go back to his Englisch life in the near future? Miriam will suffer losing him all over again and I... I have no bearing on this matter, although I'd be lying if I didn't say that I cared.*

I don't want to care for him, Gott. I don't mind feeling neighborly and kind towards him, but the feelings I have are not neighborly. And they don't want to go away. Help me Gott. Help me harden my heart against falling in love. Help me be courageous and strong for Miriam when the time comes for him to leave. I ask you this, Gott, because I know only you can lead the blind. Amen."

Lavina stood up and tried to find something to do. Anything to keep her mind of the rambling thoughts that had taken residence inside her. She was about to scoop some feed out for the chickens when a bible verse came to mind.

PSALM 37:3 Trust the Lord and do good, live in the land, and farm faithfulness.

Lavina walked out of the barn and her eyes fell on the fields of strawberries. Hope washed over her like a blanket of calm and peace as another verse came to mind.

ISAIAH 40:11 He gently leads his flock to calm waters

With that verse, Lavina realized she might not understand what had led Aaron to their door, but she had to have faith in the Lord that he had led Aaron home.

It was not her choosing whether Aaron and Miriam should've reunited, but the Lord's. Just like it hadn't been her choosing to lose her parents in the fire.

Lavina remembered how Miriam had consoled her back then, telling her that everything happened for Gott's reason. Now she simply had to have faith that once again Gott's reason was at play.

All she could do to protect herself and Miriam from the fallout that today might bring in the future was to find her strength in the Lord and harden her heart against falling even deeper in love with a man that would leave.

She only feared that when he did, he would take Miriam's joy and her heart with him.

Chapter 18
Journey's End

In the days that followed, Aaron realized the harvest season was ending. Every day they had less and fewer strawberries to harvest.

It was as if nature was telling him that his life on the road had to end as well. He had finally received the answers he had been looking for. He had found the woman that had given him life and had forgiven her for giving him up for adoption.

Aaron understood now that not only had it not been her choice, but had she kept him, he would've lived a life of shame instead of the childhood of acceptance and love. It was hard for him to understand that the Amish that could be so generous and kind could also be so cruel to an unwed mother, but he accepted it.

He had also come to accept that if he told his parents, they would feel as if they failed him in some way. They had given him everything he had ever needed; they had showered him with love and a wonderful childhood, and he wouldn't take that from them by revealing he knew the truth.

Instead, he would appreciate their love and kindness even more because of it.

As for the rest of his life, Aaron wasn't sure what he wanted from it, but he knew he couldn't put off thinking about his own future much longer.

For the last five years, he had procrastinated his studies and his future in the hopes finding out about his past. Now that he had, he knew it was time to make some decisions.

It was time to decide what he wanted from his future. It was time to decide who he wanted to be and where he wanted to spend the rest of his life. Would he spend it in Boston to be close to his parents, or would he spend it somewhere completely different to carve out a life for himself separate from the mother that had given him up unwillingly and the parents that had tried to compensate for their secret by spoiling him as a child?

The one thing Aaron knew was that he wouldn't be able to make these decisions while he was staying on the Gerber farm.

He had considered it and finally decided that he had no choice but to say goodbye to Miriam and Lavina and head back to Boston.

His heart was heavy at the thought of saying goodbye to Miriam, but it felt almost broken at the thought of saying goodbye to Lavina.

Over the last five weeks, Aaron cared for Lavina more than he had cared for any other girl in his past. He respected and adore her and wished more than anything that they could stay in touch.

But Aaron knew that wouldn't be possible.

Just like he wouldn't have been accepted as a child born out of wedlock in a society that lived by the ordnung and its expectations, he couldn't start a relationship with an Amish girl, knowing it would harm her future and her reputation.

If you love her, set her free...

The words had been repeating themselves to Aaron repeatedly. He now realized for the first time in his life that loving someone and keeping them close wasn't hard. It was letting them go.

It was because he loved Lavina that he needed to leave as well.

He couldn't trust that his feelings wouldn't grow or that he wouldn't act on them if he stayed longer.

He waited until dinner, gathering all his courage, before he broached the subject.

As if knowing he was going to say goodbye, Miriam had cooked his favorite meal since coming to the Gerber farm. Meatloaf and roast potatoes.

The scent of meatloaf and roast potatoes hung in the air as they said their silent prayers. For a moment Aaron tried to soak up the scents, the sounds and the peace surrounding him, hoping it would stay with him for the rest of his life.

He wasn't yet sure where his life was going to take him, but he knew he would never forget his time with Miriam and Lavina.

"I have an announcement to make," Aaron began when they had finished saying their prayers. Something Aaron had also begun doing every morning and every night. He found peace in knowing that the Lord was looking out for him, his faith renewed because the Lord had led him to Miriam without him even realizing it.

"It's time for you to leave, isn't it?" Miriam asked quietly, as if she had read his mind.

Aaron nodded. "The season is almost over and it's been… it's been a very long time since I've been home."

"We've appreciated your help on the farm more than you'll ever know," Miriam said with a warm smile.

Aaron's chest ached, knowing it was going to be harder than ever before to leave a town or a farm.

"Back to Boston?" Lavina asked, pushing a piece of potato around on her plate. "When do you leave?"

Aaron hated he could hear the pain in her voice. He wasn't sure if it was because he was leaving and she cared about him, or because she wouldn't have his help with the rest of the harvest.

"Tomorrow, if that's all right with you. Yes, Boston. I think it's time I decided what I want to do with my life."

"A doctor or a lawyer?" Miriam asked with a smile.

"Probably." Aaron shrugged. Although he wouldn't admit that neither of those felt right. Neither of those felt like the right fit for him, but he would think more about that on the long bus ride home.

"Those are both gut careers for an Englishman," Lavina commented.

The way she said *Englishman* emphasized the canyon of differences between them. He wished they weren't all that different.

"Yes, they are," Aaron commented, his appetite also gone.

"I'll pack you lunch for the road. The bus leaves mid-morning I think, isn't that right Lavina?" Miriam asked, turning to Lavina.

Lavina looked up with a smile, her eyes hollow. "Jah, that's right."

Aaron summoned a smile, but he couldn't help but wonder if the hollow feeling in his heart would ever disappear.

Chapter 19
A Leg Healed &
a Heart Broken

"I'm glad to report your leg has completely healed," the doctor announced as he looked at the X-rays. "You'll have a little weakness in your leg for quite some time after the cast is removed, but I'm happy to say you'll be back to your old self in no time at all."

"That's gut news," Miriam said with relief.

"Very gut news," Lavina agreed as she glanced at the clock on the wall. She knew that patience was a virtue, but she was finding it hard to be patient when she had a two entire rows of strawberries that still needed to be watered today.

It was exactly a week since Aaron had left and every day Lavina had fallen a little more behind. Between the watering, harvesting, and chores that needed to be done, it felt like she simply didn't have enough hands.

And regardless of the doctor's assurance that Miriam would be back on her feet in no time at all, she didn't want Miriam overdoing her recovery. She needed to heal and give her leg the time needed to rest after the fracture.

"I'll just get the nurse to remove the cast and then you'll be on your way." The doctor dropped his gloves in a disposal bin before leaving Lavina and Miriam alone.

"Denke for coming today. I could've really called for an Englisch driver," Miriam said as if reading Lavina's mind.

"Of course I came. I wouldn't have let you come on your own," Lavina assured her.

"I know that, but I also know that you've been out in the fields from dawn and that you go back after dinner every night to work. You'll burn out if you continue working these hours Lavina, the strawberries aren't the be all and end all of our lives." Miriam's voice was laced with concern.

Lavina glanced down at her hands and the callouses that had appeared there over the last week. A heavy sigh escaped her. "We managed before and we'll manage again."

"We will," Miriam agreed. "But for now, we need to accept that this is going to be our best season yet. I can't very well sit in that living room one more day and see you working your fingers to the bone."

"I haven't…" Lavina argued.

"I can see how the work is bearing down on you. I don't think I've seen you smile once, or even look happy." Miriam sighed heavily. "I can't help but wish that Aaron had stayed a little longer."

Lavina was about to agree, but she quickly bit back the words. She couldn't allow herself to admit that she missed him. She couldn't allow herself to consider she felt heartbroken since he had left for Boston.

She had no right to develop feelings for him in the first place, and it was no use fawning over those feelings now.

They would disappear. in time—at least, that is what she hoped for.

But Miriam didn't know how she felt. Miriam also didn't know that since Aaron had left, she had barely slept. Because every night when she climbed into bed, her thoughts turned to Aaron.

Had he decided what he wanted to become? Was he happy in Boston?

She wondered if he missed them at all.

If he missed her.

A heavy sigh escaped her as she turned to Miriam. "I…"

Just as she was about to reveal her secret to Miriam, the door opened and a nurse walked in with a small mechanical blade. "Let's get that cast off."

"You were saying, dear?" Miriam asked.

Lavina summoned a smile. "I was about to say that I'm happy your leg has healed."

"Me too, Lavina." Miriam smiled warmly. "Me too."

Lavina couldn't help but wonder if her broken heart would ever heal. She had never felt this way about a man before and with Aaron having stolen her heart, she wondered if she ever would again.

Chapter 20
Daunting Decisions

"Aaron, I can't express to you how glad we are to have you home," Sally Richards said as she sat down in the living room.

An interior decorator had designed the entire space. Before he came back from the farm, the opulence had never occurred to him. The white marble and grey sofas were beautiful, but not functional at all.

As he stood by the doors to the patio, he longed for a view of strawberry vines instead of upscale houses and skyscrapers in the distance.

"Your mother is right. Although we weren't that fond of the idea of you travelling across the country working as a second-rate immigrant, we are grateful that you learned the value of hard work," Angus Richards stated, as he handed his wife a glass of wine.

"Your father mentioned you wanted to talk to us. We can only imagine that you've finally chosen an alma mater," his mother said excitedly.

"Harvard, right, son?" Angus asked, holding up his glass, ready to make a toast.

"Actually," Aaron drew in a deep breath and summoned all his courage. If he had thought confronting Miriam about the adoption was hard, he hadn't even considered how hard this conversation would be. "Dad, can I have a soda?"

Ever since he had returned from Zook's Corner, Aaron couldn't stop thinking about Lavina. At first, he had been so excited to start his new life and to choose a career, but with every day that passed, he felt more and more lost in the *Englisch* world as Lavina would call it.

He found there was too much noise, too much ambition, too much pretense and most of all he missed the contentment of a hard day's work. Today when he had simply wanted to water the garden to clear his mind, the Gardner had quickly insisted it wasn't necessary.

For the first time, Aaron wondered why his parents never watered the garden themselves.

"You were saying?" his father asked as he handed him a soda.

"I want you both to know that I'm grateful for everything you've done for me. You've given me every privilege I can imagine. I've never wanted for love, food, or comfort and for that I will be forever grateful."

Sally chuckled. "Goodness, Aaron, you sound as if you're writing an obituary."

"I'm not, but there is something I have to tell you. I know you might be angry and that you might feel rejected, but I need you to know that I love you regardless of how you react." Aaron drew in a deep breath and met his father's gaze before turning to his mother.

He knew he was about to shatter their world, but he couldn't go on living a lie.

Chapter 21
A New Beginning

"It feels so gut to be in the sun again!" Miriam called out from a few rows over.

"Just be careful. I can't carry you back to the house if you exhaust yourself," Lavina called back with an indulgent smile.

It had been almost a month since the cast had come off and today was the first time Miriam had come out to help in the fields. Until now she had done her daily exercises and moved between the house and the barn, but Lavina had been firm about her staying out of the fields.

A late drenching of rain in the season seemed to have given the strawberries a new life. Just when Lavina had thought they were done harvesting for the season, new fruit sprouted on the vines. The extra produce overjoyed Lavina, but the work was getting to her.

Without Miriam or Aaron's help, she felt exhausted at night. It also didn't help that she still thought of Aaron most nights before fatigue finally won her over.

"Exhaust myself—I'm feeling renewed. I needed this just as much as you need the help," Miriam called back.

Lavina laughed. She had assigned Miriam to harvesting the fruit that was ready, while she watered the strawberries row by row.

As she picked up the ladling spoon, it took her back to the day she and Aaron had played and laughed in the fields. She was almost certain that was the day she had fallen in love with him.

Even after a month, she still felt her heart ache when she thought of him. She couldn't help but regret that she hadn't asked him to write, or at least to keep in touch.

Instead, Aaron had become a memory, just like her parents, and in time the memories would fade. Her eyes stung with tears, tears she had refused to cry since Aaron had left. It was foolish to cry for a man that didn't care for you in return.

When he had left, hardly saying a single word, it had convinced Lavina that the feelings she had developed for Aaron had been one-sided. She wasn't sure what hurt more. To know that she had fallen in love with a man that didn't love her back? Or to know that she had fallen in love with a man that loved her and left.

Either way, it had broken her heart.

"You've done a splendid job, Lavina. These vines are strong and healthy. I couldn't have done it better myself," Miriam called out proudly.

Lavina smiled at Miriam over the rows of strawberries. "I had a lot of help. Aaron has a green thumb and a delicate touch."

"I hope he's doing well. I'm so glad he found me," Miriam said almost to herself.

Lavina didn't reply, not trusting herself not to cry if she spoke of Aaron anymore. They finished the rest of their work in silence. By the time they were headed back to the barn to start on the afternoon chores, an Englisch car pulled into the yard.

"Are you expecting anyone?" Lavina asked Miriam with a furrowed brow.

"Not at all," Miriam said, shaking her head as she leaned against the barn door for support.

"Is your leg all right?" Lavina asked, forgetting about the car and rushing to Miriam's side.

"Good heavens, if it isn't, I'll tell you. Now go see who that…." Miriam's jaw dropped mid-sentence.

Lavina turned to see the cause of Miriam's shock, when she felt her own jaw drop even as her eyes widened with surprise.

It wasn't an Englischer climbing out of the car, instead it was an Amish man. An Amish man that smiled at her in the way Aaron had done for all those weeks.

Her heart skipped a beat even as her breath caught in her chest. "Aaron?"

Miriam laughed. "You're right, that's Aaron."

He handed money to the driver before he turned to Lavina and Miriam with a shrug and a smile. "I hope you still need a seasonal hand, because I'm kind of hoping for room and board."

Lavina couldn't be more shocked if someone had told her that her strawberries had turned blue overnight.

Miriam and Lavina listened to Aaron as he explained he was back. But this time not as a seasonal hand that wanted to leave at the end of the season, this time as a prospective member of the community.

Miriam was overjoyed. She hugged her son and praised the Lord before she insisted on heading to the house to start on dinner. Before she could leave, Aaron called her back.

"There is another reason I've decided to become Amish." Aaron turned to Lavina and searched her gaze. "From the first moment I met you, Lavina. I knew you were different. At first, I thought it was the divide between Amish and Englisch, but I soon realized it was your heart. Your strength, wisdom, faith, and courage made me admire you and…. Fall in love with you."

Miriam gasped. "Lavina?"

Lavina felt tears constricting her throat. "Aaron I…"

"Please let me finish first. I returned to the city with plans of going to college and starting a career. But I found the city too loud, the people too shallow, and I found it lacking you. You taught me how to pray and, without realizing it, you taught me how to love. You taught me you can find contentment in the smallest of things and joy in the most unexpected. I don't know if you feel the same way, and if you don't, I won't blame you. But I want you to know that as soon as I'm baptized, I plan on courting you. I want to spend the rest of my life learning from you," Aaron finished with a hopeful smile.

All the emotions Lavina had tried to hide for so long, the feelings she had suppressed, all came bubbling to the surface. "Ach, Aaron, I fell in love with you too. I was afraid my heart would never heal after you left…"

"How did I not notice any of this?" Miriam asked, pretending to be angry.

Lavina turned to Miriam with a warm smile. "Because sometimes a woman learns how to keep a secret so close to her heart that no one will ever guess it."

"But I no longer want it to be a secret," Aaron announced. "I've already spent the first three weeks of my proving period on the bishop's farm. With his approval, I can continue my proving period here, working for you... that's... if you'll have me."

Lavina and Miriam looked at each other before they both burst out laughing. "Welcome back, Aaron."

Miriam left them to start on dinner, understanding they needed a moment alone. As soon as she was out of earshot, Aaron moved towards Lavina. He framed her face and smiled into her eyes. "Do you realize that I felt lost all these years? I went on a search for my birth mother only to discover that I really needed to find you. I plan on spending my life showing you how much I love you."

Lavina leaned into his hand. "I plan on never trying to steal my heart back again. It's yours."

With the sun setting over the strawberry fields, Lavina realized it didn't matter what happened in life, Gott was in control.

His faith had guided her to this moment, his strength had kept her going during the toughest of times, and his blessings of love had made it all worth it.

*** The End ***

Thank you kindly for choosing to read my book. I sincerely hope you enjoyed it. All of my Amish Romances are wholesome stories suitable for all to enjoy.

If you could be so kind to leave a review on Amazon, I would appreciate it.